T0354731

Inside
Religion

Inside
Religion

Jane Doe

Archway Publishing books may be ordered through booksellers or by contacting:

Archway Publishing
1663 Liberty Drive
Bloomington, IN 47403
www.archwaypublishing.com
844-669-3957

Scripture quotations are taken from World English Bible, public domain.

ISBN: 978-1-6657-6003-4 (sc)
ISBN: 978-1-6657-6004-1 (e)

Library of Congress Control Number: 2024909592

Print information available on the last page.

Archway Publishing rev. date: 08/23/2024

True religion is being undefiled before God.

—Rev. W. Mark Sexson

CONTENTS

ONE

The Interview

"You know, you can't legally ask me that," Stuart Jones said, rather more forcefully than he intended. He really wanted this job. Well, he didn't really want *this* particular job. He wanted to get a foot in the door at the *Times*, and he was certain this was his chance.

"Of course, I can ask you that," Henry Carter responded. "If you are applying for the religion editor position, I need to know if you can relate to our readers. An atheist wouldn't relate very well to readers of the religion section. 'What religion do you affiliate with?' is a fair question and directly relates to the ability to do your job."

Henry Carter, editor in chief, stood across the desk and looked at a younger version of himself from thirty years ago. He knew very well he shouldn't ask this young punk what church he attended, but he was trying to see if he believed in something other than himself before he gave him the job. He was well acquainted with his work because he had viewed his portfolio. Really, he was the only candidate who could string two sentences together when compared with the rubbish he read from other candidates.

"I wouldn't call myself an atheist, actually," Stuart replied, "but I think being unaffiliated with any particular religion would make me more relatable to all religions. There wouldn't be any preconceived ideas standing in the way of my reporting."

He has a point, thought Henry. "What experience do you have with budgeting and working advertising campaigns?"

"I have limited experience, as you probably know if you read my résumé." Stuart wondered what kind of budget he would have or if he would have to come up with what he needed by getting advertisers. He couldn't help noticing the portrait hanging on the wall behind the editor. He wondered if it was his wife or daughter. *She is certainly beautiful*, he thought. From what he learned about the crusty old man, it was probably his daughter. He wasn't the type to have an arm-candy wife at his age, unlike some other media moguls.

"Speaking of your résumé," Henry said, "what were you doing from 2003 to 2007? Those years are missing."

"I was in the Army," Stuart replied tersely. He didn't like to talk about his service in the Special Forces, especially to the elite class of snobs who looked down their noses from their ivory towers where fake news lived. That was one reason he was trying to get hired at *The Times*—to write the truth and get politics out of real reporting. He wasn't sure if he would be allowed to strip the spin out of his stories, but he wanted to try. At least when writing for the religion section, few elites would pay that close attention. Besides, his service wasn't exactly finished; he might get called up should there be another event like 9/11. *Once in the unit, always in the unit*, he thought.

"Thank you for your service," Henry said. "I was in 'Nam, myself. Where'd you serve overseas?"

"Mostly Afghanistan," came the reply. "Getting back to the budget, will I have to raise what I need, or are there some funds for a secretary or research?"

Doesn't like to talk about his service, Henry thought. *Hmmm, probably means he was or is Special Forces.* Henry cleared his throat and said, "You share staff reporters and a secretary with the travel section.

They bring in more advertising dollars, so you will have to raise some advertising dollars. They also have a daily section. You will only have Saturdays. You'll also be expected to write about local news and events approximately once a week. But it may be more if filler is needed. You can start on those and build up a stash so the city editor can pull from your file when extra filler is needed. As an editor, you will need to have two to three columns ready each week. You can also have an intern to help you with any research needed."

"I would like to research what religions are represented by the city and state's population and write about each faith in depth without political bias. Perhaps it will remind people what is important about their faith, and they will learn about other faiths as well. I'll check with the secretary and writers about advertising options," Stuart said, hoping he sounded confident.

"The secretary has been here awhile and can be a little abrupt," Henry said. "But Mrs. B's bark is worse than her bite. I'd maybe ask her what kind of donuts she likes first, though."

"So, I have the job?" Stuart asked.

"When can you start?" Henry responded.

"Now," Stuart said a little too enthusiastically.

"Well, why don't you wait until Monday? That is the first of the month and first of the week. You can take a little time to formulate your new plan for the religion section," Henry replied, sticking out his hand for Stuart to shake.

"Thank you," Stuart said pumping Henry's hand. Without thinking, he blurted out, "If my daughter was as beautiful as that, I wouldn't hang her picture behind me where I couldn't see it all the time." *Damn,* he thought, *why did I say that?*

"See you Monday." Henry smiled, sat down, and turned to his computer. *Damn,* he thought, *he has a point.* He thought of his late wife. *That is something you would have pointed out, Naomi.*

T W O

The Daughter

"Hi, Dad," Jennifer Carter answered her phone while shuffling the boxes she was trying to get down off the shelf. They tumbled to the floor, spilling their contents all over.

"What was that sound?" Henry Carter asked.

"I dropped some of the boxes from Mom's closet shelf," Jennifer replied.

"How is it coming, Jen? Thank you for helping me go through her things." Henry thought to himself, *It has been long enough.* Naomi Carter, wife of Henry, mother of Jennifer, and dazzler of both their worlds succumbed to cancer two years earlier, following a long and arduous battle, which left everyone dead, either literally or figuratively. Neither Jennifer nor her father was able to accomplish much other than putting one foot in front of the other to get to work or school. And neither was willing to make the other face the reality that their lives really did have to go on without their loved one.

"Well, I got a late start today, so I'm only on her closet in the guest room," Jennifer said. She sat down on the floor to look at the contents that were scattered there. She thought, *I'm glad I took this year off school. It is going to take forever to go through all her stuff. I can't believe she never threw anything away.*

"I hired the religion editor today," Henry told Jennifer as he was taking down her portrait from behind his desk. "I was calling to see if you might want to put in a couple hours a day to help him with research. You are a whiz at computer searches."

"Why does a religion editor need to do research?" she asked. She wasn't really paying attention to the conversation because she was unwrapping the toilet-paper-covered figurines.

"Not really sure, other than he said he was going to take politics out of the stories he writes. So maybe he needs to look up a few facts," Henry continued. "Why don't you come by for lunch on Monday, and I'll introduce you. I feel bad that you felt the need to take a year off school."

"Dad, we've been over this before," Jennifer reminded him. "I wasn't doing well in school and didn't want to waste your money. It is going to take me awhile to get through Mom's belongings. Are you sure you want to donate everything? She has some nice things."

"We talked about this before," Henry said, gently chiding his daughter. "You keep whatever you want and donate the rest. I want it to go to a good cause."

They hung up. Henry busied himself with hanging up his daughter's picture on the wall opposite his desk so that he could see it as he was working. *Someday,* he thought, *she will leave me too. She will find a husband and have a family of her own.* Having accomplished his task, he sat down to review the reports on his desk. He shut the door and blinds, turned on the smoke evacuator, and lit up his favorite cigar.

Jennifer, on the other hand, grabbed a can of diet soda and her laptop. She was going to see what these figurines were worth. She noticed the date of "1935" printed on the bottom of one particularly pretty ceramic child with a trumpet and thought she could make out the word "Leipzig" on the tag strung around the base.

"Hi, Mrs. B!" Jennifer called out as she made her way to her dad's office.

"Jennifer, honey," Mrs. B called back, "you're in for a real treat!"

"What do you mean?" Jennifer stopped, turned, and looked at her questioningly.

"I met that cute religion editor Stuart. I already asked if he is married, and he isn't. He might not be your type, though. He isn't Ivy League and doesn't have a Martha's Vineyard connection."

Jennifer felt her cheeks go pink. "Mrs. B, I hope you didn't say anything about me."

"He asked me what my favorite donut was," Mrs. B smiled smugly. "I might not be too hard on him."

"Mrs. B, you are hard on everybody," Jennifer said, laughing. She knocked on her father's office door and went in without waiting for a reply. "Where's my picture?" Jennifer asked as soon as she opened the door.

"Hi, Jen," Henry replied. "Turn around. I moved it so that I could look at you from my desk."

"Ahh, that's something Mom would have suggested," Jennifer said, giving her father a kiss on the cheek. "So where is this new religion editor Mrs. B is babbling on about?" She heard someone clear his throat and turned around to glimpse the most gorgeous guy she had ever seen. He was tall and muscular. He had dark piercing eyes, olive-tanned skin, and wavy black hair, and he was staring at her. No, he was staring through her. Then his cheeks lifted into a smile, and his eyes melted her insides. She opened and shut her mouth, not wanting to say something stupid. *Yikes,* she thought, *I better be careful with this one.*

"Stuart Jones," he said, reaching out to shake her hand. "You're every bit as beautiful as your portrait."

"Jennifer," was all she was able to croak out in response. *Breathe, you idiot!* She could see her dad out of the corner of her eye. He had a bemused expression on his face. She turned away and forced herself to say, "Nice to meet you, Stuart. So, my dad says you could use some help with research."

"Let's discuss this over lunch," Henry Carter suggested as he moved toward the door to usher them out. He winked at his daughter as she passed him, and she rolled her eyes.

THREE

The Plan

"Okay, let's get started," Stuart directed as he made his way to the front of the conference room. The stuffy room in the corner of the newsroom had only one small window. It was in need of a new paint job. It was rarely used due to the fact that so many people worked in the field or connected remotely to meetings. Stuart wanted to meet everyone who would be working in the religion section. Thus, he requested this meeting to begin his career as a newspaper column editor. *Even though it is only the religion section,* he thought.

"Why don't we go around the room and introduce ourselves. Let's say something about ourselves that is relevant to our positions here at the newspaper? I'll go first," Stuart continued. "Stuart Jones, recent graduate from Saint John's College in Annapolis. Spent some time in the military prior to university. It is my goal to beef up the religion section so that it sells more weekend papers and perhaps gets the readers to think a bit more about religion or reconnect with it if they have lapsed in their belief. Certainly, we want to sell more newspapers to make this section profitable and thus create more room for inspirational stories. Enid and Abe, I know you have written religion pieces for several years, and they are well written. I just want to take the politics out. Let's be more relevant to our local readers without any political slant. Does that make sense?"

"I'll go next," Enid answered. "Enid Jeffery, part-time writer. To be honest, I despise writing about religion. I prefer covering the weather, travel, or anything else but the Pope or the Sunnis killing Shiites. I worked at Random House as a travel book editor for about twenty years until I decided to work less when my husband retired. I've been here about five years. To be honest, I don't think your plan will work, but I am willing to try it. Just don't expect me to attend church bazaars or travel to Mecca." Everyone in the room laughed at that.

"Abe Hoffman." Abe spoke up next. "I might be the only religious person here. I am a rabbi for a small synagogue just off Main and 17th. I have been contributing articles for quite some time—mainly every time Israel elects a new prime minister, or a new war breaks out in the Middle East. I also work part-time at the chamber of commerce, so I think I bring a lot to the local travel section. Enid and I complement each other in that I love writing about religion. I like your idea of taking politics out of the news. I can go back to being a teacher."

Stuart smiled and said, "Thank you, Abe. I asked Jerry Chang from accounting to be here at this initial meeting to offer his opinion about the changes required for us to be profitable. Jerry, you're up next."

"Hi, folks," Jerry said. "I've been here about forty years. I started as a delivery boy and then graduated to the circulation department. I've been in accounting for the last ten years. I can remember when all the churches and synagogues used to advertise in the paper and list the times of their religious services. Now I'm not sure if they even do that in the online paper. That's a different department. The reason I bring this up is that travel covers their print costs by selling approximately $30,000 in advertising per month. Their big section is printed on Sundays. They have an average of a three-column width daily. Your section is only printed on Saturdays, but you guys don't bring in any advertising dollars anymore, which is why you're limited to about a two-to-three column width each week. If you could knock on some church doors and get them to advertise again, you could probably expand up to your own page."

"Let me stop you there, Jerry," Stuart interrupted. "There are about 2,500 places of worship in the greater metro area, so if we were to get 10 percent to spend a hundred dollars a month in advertising, would that be enough?"

"Probably," Jerry answered. "You have a good team here. You can get inventive."

"I'll go next," Mrs. B. piped up. "Martha Brooks, but you already know to call me Mrs. B. I've been here longer than anyone, even your dad, Jennifer." She turned to smile at Jennifer and then back to the room. She continued, "I used to answer calls, but now it is mostly answering email requests. They are all travel related. I can't remember the last time I had a religion-related request or call. I keep track of hours. If anything needs to be mailed, I take care of that. Accounting takes care of invoicing advertisers. Occasionally, I have to do a setup for a new advertiser to get approval, but that is rare these days. I can make phone calls to see what kind of response we will get from the places of worship."

Stuart interjected, saying, "Let's dive into the old newspaper copies in the morgue and see what kinds of ads used to be placed in the paper. And can you get with the online department to see if any church or synagogue advertises online?"

"I can help with that too," Jennifer piped in. "I'm Jennifer; Jen or Jenny for short. My dad is the editor in chief and asked me to help with some research for the changes to the religion section. I'm taking this year off from school. I like what Stuart is proposing. Maybe it will interest the segment of population who quit reading *The Times*."

Jennifer continued, saying, "I wonder if we could offer a free ad to the churches who advertise every month—a small space to advertise a special service or holiday schedule."

"That might get them on board if they have the budget," Jerry said as he nodded his assent to Jennifer.

"Thank you, Jen," Stuart smiled as he turned to the whiteboard. "OK, there are fifty-two weeks in a year or twelve months. There are about five-to-six major world religions and a handful of Asian religions that we may or may not want to independently highlight depending on the demographics of the city and state. I thought I would start out by describing what we hope to accomplish in whatever space we are given in the first week. Let's try to get the advisers on board within the first month so that the money coming in will free more column space. Then we will highlight each religion, major holidays, and human-interest stories." On a notebook, he wrote, "Christianity, Islam, Hinduism, Buddhism, Sikhism, Judaism, Asian religions."

"Jennifer, can you see what you can find about the current religious preferences for the population in the city and state?" Stuart asked. Abe raised his hand. "Yes, Abe?"

"I wonder if we should divide Christianity into Catholic and Protestant? We could even do an article on the reformation in November."

"That makes sense," Stuart said. "Abe, Enid, and Mrs. B. can get started on finding the contact information of the city's places of worship to build our database."

Jennifer raised her hand. "Yes, Jen." Stuart smiled again.

"I wonder if we should make appointments to meet with the clergy of each religion to get familiar with it firsthand?" Jennifer said.

"That's a very good plan," Stuart said as he continued to smile at Jennifer. Everyone looked at her and then at Stuart.

FOUR

The City

"Catholics," Abe announced as they hunched over their lunches in the conference room. It was in response to Stuart's question about what the largest religious group in the wider metro area was. "Then Protestants, Jews, Muslims, Hindis, and Buddhists. I guess we can group all Christians together, but it might be worthwhile to write about Catholics and Protestants separately."

Two weeks after the initial launch, they were meeting again. They had already gotten a hundred places of worship committed to advertising on their Saturday religion page. It took some convincing on Stuart's part to include free online ads. Cyberspace is much cheaper than paper space. It didn't hurt that Jennifer had been influential in her father's making the decision. As it was, the revenue would start. A hundred entries would take up half the page. It would be a worship directory containing the name, address, phone numbers, and service times of each faith.

"How does that compare to the US national affiliations?" Stuart asked.

"Flip the Catholics with Protestants, and the others fall into about the same order," Abe responded. "I wouldn't publish any firm numbers, as we were looking at reports from various years. We've got a pretty good idea of the city's religious views. Some of the data was rather surprising in that it showed the younger population having more 'none' responses as to religious affiliation."

"How are you doing on setting up meetings with the clergy, Jen?" Stuart asked as he sat down next to her with his sandwich and cup of coffee.

"Well," she answered, "I've made about a dozen calls to date, and no one has called me back. I'll try again. We have a rabbi right here. We can start with the Jewish faith and interview Abe. I don't know why I didn't think of that before. Would that be okay, Abe?" she asked.

"Fine with me," Abe replied, "but I'm not really a scholar. You may want to interview someone more familiar with Jewish history."

"You would make a better subject for what I am trying to achieve because you are with your flock, so to speak," Stuart interjected. "I want to write about what people believe about their faith. I'm putting the finishing touches on my initial article that introduces the updated religion section. Anyone want to read it when I get done?" Stuart asked. Everyone stopped eating and looked at Stuart. After the silence stretched to an uncomfortable interval, Stuart said, "What?"

"You're the editor, Stuart," Enid told him. "You should be reading our work, not the other way around. But I would be happy to read it if you like."

"Ah, well, it's just that I want it to be effective. The readership probably will pass it by and head for the crossword anyway."

"Why don't you come to Shabbat this Saturday?" Abe asked. "Services start at 10:00 a.m."

"I'll go," Jennifer said. "Meet you there?" she asked Stuart.

"Well, okay," Stuart responded. Everyone else declined and left to get back to their computers.

When they were alone, Jennifer asked Stuart, "Have you ever been to a church service?"

"I was at my uncle's funeral. Does that count?" Stuart said.

"Well, I suppose so," she said, thinking about her mom's funeral. "I didn't mean to put you on the spot with Abe. You don't have to go if you don't want to. I've never been to a Jewish service. I wonder if they get many believers outside of the faith attending services."

"I guess you can count the chaplain's service when I was overseas in the military, but they were rather watered down. I could have just as easily been attending a Rotary Club meeting," Stuart replied.

"Have you ever been to a Rotary Club meeting?" Jennifer asked, smiling.

Stuart laughed, "Well, no, but I can imagine what they are like after sitting through a chaplain's service. I just can't imagine how there can be so many beliefs and faiths, especially now that science explains away many natural phenomena. The ancient civilizations had a god for everything they couldn't explain."

"And now there is one God," Jennifer said quietly. "At least, that is what I believe. How else can you explain the absolute miracle of life in the expanse of the solar system?"

"We aren't going to answer that one in our column, I'm afraid," Stuart said. "Have you always lived in the city?" He wanted to change the subject.

"Since I was in the third grade," she responded. "We lived in Germany before that. Dad was a war correspondent for Reuters."

"I've spent some time in Germany," he said. "I've only lived here in the city about three weeks. Maybe you can show me around your favorite places?" he asked, hoping he didn't sound too eager.

She felt herself blush and turned away, saying, "Sure, we can start after Abe's meeting. I need to get back to the phones."

"Yeah," Stuart said, fidgeting with his pen, "I'll talk to you later."

FIVE

The Questions

Inside Religion
Stuart Jones, Editor
(For publication Saturday, June 11, 2011)

Hello, readers,

We are changing the religion section of *The Times*. As editor, I hope you will find it educational and enjoyable. Let me be honest with you. I am not a very religious person, and I know very little about most religions, so I hope to learn with you about the different religions in our city. It is my hope that this knowledge will lead to a greater understanding of the different cultures represented by the various religions.

Did you know there are more than 2,500 institutions of faith in the greater metro area? When the city was founded, there were only three: Dutch Reformed, French Protestant, and Lutheran. Over the centuries, immigrants brought new religions and customs and made this the most culturally diverse city in the world. It has only been within the last few decades that religious affiliations started to decline.

The First Amendment in the Bill of Rights reads, "Congress shall make no law respecting an establishment of religion, or prohibiting the free exercise thereof, or abridging the freedom of speech, or of the press; or the right of the people peaceably to assemble, and to petition the Government for a redress of grievances." The founding fathers themselves were very religious, and they understood the necessity and absolute liberty of allowing citizens to practice religion as they chose. Benjamin Franklin, signer of the Declaration of Independence and the Constitution of the United States, wrote just a few years after the founding of the country:

Here is my Creed. I believe in one God, the Creator of the Universe. That He governs it by His Providence. That He ought to be worshipped. That the most acceptable service we render to him is in doing good to his other children. That the soul of man is immortal, and will be treated with justice in another life respecting its conduct in this. These I take to be the fundamental points in all sound religion, and I regard them as you do in whatever sect I meet with them.[1]

Thomas Jefferson, founding father from Virginia and primary author of the Declaration of Independence, wrote these words in a letter just two years prior to his presidency:

I am for freedom of religion, & against all maneuvres [sic] to bring about a legal ascendancy of one sect over another.[2]

George Washington wrote in his farewell address:

Of all the dispositions and habits which lead to political prosperity, religion and morality are indispensable supports. In vain would that man claim the tribute of patriotism, who should labor to subvert these great pillars of human happiness, these firmest props of the duties of men and citizens. The mere politician, equally with the pious man, ought to respect and to cherish them. A volume could not trace all their connections with private and public felicity. Let it simply be asked: Where is the security for property, for reputation, for life, if the sense of religious obligation desert the oaths which are the instruments of investigation in courts of justice?[3]

John Adams, second president of the United States, believed our form of government depended on religious people. He said,

Our Constitution was made only for a moral and religious people. It is wholly inadequate to the government of any other.[4]

The importance of religion was deeply embedded in America's founding. And 234 years later, President Obama reminded us of religious liberty when he said,

This is America. And our commitment to religious freedom must be unshakeable. The principle that peoples of all faiths are welcome in this country, and will not be treated differently by their government, is essential to who we are.[5]

I believe the recent decline in religious affiliations correlates to the increase in depression, civil unrest, and violence in communities across the nation, which is why I want to lead you, the reader, inside the religions of our city. This column will share information obtained from faith leaders in the greater metro area. It is my hope that you will do one of two things. First, if you relate to it, I hope it will rekindle seeds of faith and take you back to a church, synagogue, temple, or mosque. Second, if you don't relate, I hope you will gain understanding about the beliefs of others and learn to live by the Golden Rule.

The questions I will discuss with faith leaders include:

- How was the religion founded?
- What are the core beliefs?
- What is the worship style?
- What does your religion require of you?
- What are its views on life after death?

I hope that you will have your own questions and that you will seek out your clergy for the answers.

Stuart Jones, editor

SIX

The Rabbi

"Shabbat! Shalom!" everyone around Jennifer and Stuart responded at the end of the service. People were milling around and talking to each other as they slowly made their way out of the temple.

"Well, what did you think?" Jennifer asked Stuart as they were making their way to the front to speak to Abe.

"I enjoyed it. It was longer than I thought it would be," he said, looking at his watch.

"There was definitely a lot more singing and chanting than I am used to," Jennifer replied. "Hi, Abe."

"Jennifer, Stuart, great to see you. What did you think?" Abe asked, giving them both a hug.

"I was a little concerned that it was going to all be in Hebrew," Stuart lamented. "I'm glad you gave your message in English. I liked how you related a story from thousands of years ago to the community today. I especially liked how you used the Obama quote from my editorial. Or maybe you didn't read it, and it is a huge coincidence," Stuart told Abe.

"Actually, I did take a sneak peek at it. I wanted to before it prints next week," Abe said, smiling.

"Do you have time to answer a few questions?" Stuart asked.

"Sure, but let's get something to eat," Abe said as he ushered them toward the exit. "How about Manny's?" he continued.

"Ooh, that is one of my favorite restaurants," Jennifer piped in. "We can start with that as one of my favorite places." She smiled at Stuart as they headed out the door.

"How was the religion founded?" Stuart asked.

"Well, you would think it began with Adam and Eve, and it does when considering the creation of man. But really, it began when God instituted a covenant with his people," Abe said in response to Stuart's first question. "Many of Adam's descendants believed in idols and false gods. Our religion actually began with a young boy named Abram who lived in Babylon with his father, who sold idols. Abram believed there was only one God and smashed all the idols in his father's shop. God instructed Abram to leave his city, Ur, and travel to Canaan, the land of the Israelites. This marked the beginning of the Abrahamic Covenant. Abram, whose name was changed to Abraham, was promised descendants as numerous as the stars. This happened nearly four thousand years ago. I believe that we are tasked to bring mankind to the God of the Torah."

"What are your core beliefs?" Stuart asked.

"Judaism is more than a belief in one universal and eternal God, who is good and who knows each of us. The Jewish faith rests on belief in the miracles of creation and the escape from Pharaoh in the Exodus. The Ten Commandments were given to Moses and were passed down in order to make people good. We believe that the Torah is from God. This belief does not necessarily mean that it was dictated by God, but it comes from God, not men."

Jennifer asked, "What is the Torah exactly?"

"The word *Torah* literally means instruction for life," Abe answered. "It is referring to the parchment scroll version of the five books of Moses, which relate to the first five books of the Christian Bible. Important texts include Exodus 15, Deuteronomy 6, and Leviticus 19, which instruct us how to relate to God and each other. Other Jewish works of history, wisdom, and prophecy are also referred to as Torah, but the books of Moses hold a special place. The Mishnah is known as the oral Torah. They are interpretations of the Torah, which were written down about fifteen hundred years ago."

"Would you say the service we attended is representative of most Jewish worship services?" Stuart asked.

"I would say so," Abe answered. "Orthodox services are completely held in Hebrew or Yiddish. Some reformed synagogues have choirs. Of course, they are held on Saturday, so everyone can rest on Shabbat, the seventh day. The services can be very athletic—standing, sitting, standing, and sitting."

"I take it that you believe in an afterlife?" Stuart said in the form of a question.

Abe answered. "It is generally believed that there is an afterlife. God rewards the good and punishes the bad. This reward is available to all people, not just Jews. However, we choose to focus our energy and relationships in the here and now. We look for ways to interact with God and one another as a community."

"Can anyone become a Jew?" Stuart asked.

"The Jewish religion isn't about Jews," Abe said. "It is about God. If a mother is Jewish, then it is generally accepted that her children are Jewish, but anyone can convert to Judaism."

"Okay, thanks, Abe. I think this will be enough for a column," Stuart said as he was putting away the recorder and his notes. "I'm sure you will correct anything I write that may not be representative of Judaism."

"It was a pleasure," Abe answered. "I don't suppose the paper will pick up our lunch?"

They all laughed as they got up to put on their coats. They left the restaurant after Stuart paid. Abe said goodbye and headed to the nearest subway station. Jennifer and Stuart walked slowly in the opposite direction.

SEVEN

Judaism: The Covenant People

Stuart Jones, Editor
(For publication Saturday, July 9)

> "Now Yahweh said to Abram, "Leave your country, and your relatives, and your father's house, and go to the land that I will show you. I will make of you a great nation. I will bless you and make your name great. You will be a blessing. I will bless those who bless you, and I will curse him who treats you with contempt. All the families of the earth will be blessed through you."
>
> —Genesis 12:1–3

God made a covenant with Abraham to be his God, and his offspring would be God's people. The descendants of Abraham and Sarah through Isaac lead a bittersweet life in the land of Canaan until the impending famine that led them to Egypt. Once prosperous, they became enslaved by a Pharaoh who knew nothing about the good deeds Joseph rendered the Egyptians. Moses, the sixth generation and a descendant of Abraham, led the Israelites out of Egypt, through a miraculous crossing of the Red Sea, and into the desert where he received the Ten Commandments directly from God. These are found in Exodus 20:3–17, and I'll rephrase them for you.

1. You shall have no other gods before Me.
2. You shall make no idols.
3. You shall not take the name of the Lord your God in vain.
4. Keep the Sabbath day holy.
5. Honor your father and your mother.
6. You shall not murder.
7. You shall not commit adultery.
8. You shall not steal.
9. You shall not bear false witness against your neighbor.
10. You shall not covet.

These rules are the basis for living in a relationship with God for all Abrahamic faiths. They are an important part of the covenant God made with Moses and the Israelites at Mount Sinai. The Israelites, under the leadership of Joshua, entered into the Promised Land with God's help. Remembering the miraculous deeds of God and striving to live according to his commandments is the essence of being Jewish.

These commandments are as important today as they were when they were first carved in stone tablets at Mount Sinai. The followers of Judaism believe in one God, the Creator of the universe, who made the world for humankind. These rules, as well as other instructions for a good life, are found in the Torah (the five books of Moses). They are read in synagogues and at home celebrations and are put on the doorways of their homes.

The God of creation is the God of the Torah. He wants his people to be good and to love him with all their hearts, souls, strength, and minds. The Sabbath in Judaism, or Shabbat, is on Sunday, and worship services are usually on Saturday. They can be lively. They're filled with singing, recitations of Torah, messages from their rabbis, and fellowship with God's people, who strive to be moral, just, and compassionate.

An important belief of Judaism is that all people are created in the image of God. The most important distinction among human beings is not their race, religion, nationality, class, or sex, but it is their behavior. In the words of Viktor Frankl, author of *Man's Search for Meaning*, "From all this we may learn that there are only two races of men in this world, but only these two—the 'race' of the decent man and the 'race' of the indecent man."[6]

God rewards the good and punishes the bad in the afterlife. The reward in the afterlife is available to everyone, not just Jews. Thus, Judaism's primary task is to make people good by regular meetings and observances of special holy days.

The nearly thirteen million followers of Judaism live primarily in the United States and Israel. There are three major branches: Orthodox (the most traditional), Conservative, and Reformed Judaism (the least conservative). Although each branch is rooted in common beliefs, they differ in terms of scriptural interpretation and specific practices. There are nearly one hundred synagogues in the city, thus making it easy to find one where you can feel at home. Judaism can uplift anyone. Any non-Jew is welcome to embrace Judaism and become a member of the Jewish faith. No one needs to become a Jew to be saved.

EIGHT

The Buddha

Monday morning found the group back in the conference room with their cups of coffee.

"I don't know about using the word *saved*," Abe said after reading the column.

Stuart began his reply, "Well, I wanted to—"

"As a matter of fact, just take out that last sentence all together," Abe said.

"Okay," Stuart said. "I don't want it to detract from the rest of the article."

"Enid," Stuart turned to the back of the conference room. "Great articles on Ramadan and Rosh Hashanah." Turning back to Abe, Stuart said, "Will you write about Yom Kippur and Diwali?"

"On it," Abe answered.

"Jen, where are we with a Buddhist temple leader?" Stuart asked.

"I just talked to a monk from the Buddhist Vihara Center," Jennifer replied. "He can see you Wednesday morning at ten. I am still unable to connect with an imam."

"I know an imam," Stuart responded. "Not a problem."

"Mrs. B., do you have a feel for Saturday paper sales?" Stuart asked just as she bit into her donut.

Holding her finger up, she chewed and swallowed before saying, "I may be too optimistic, but I think sales are up a couple of percentage points."

"Okay, good work, everyone. Let's get busy," Stuart dismissed the group. Jennifer was the last to leave. He put his hand on her arm. The contact was electric. They both looked at his hand and then at each other. "Want to go to lunch?" Stuart asked.

"Sure," she said and smiled.

"Thank you for seeing us," Stuart told the Venerable Sarada. "I don't know very much about the Buddhist religion other than it is very old and involves meditation."

"Indeed, it is very old," the monk said. "Its origins date back to the time of Confucius, Pythagoras, and the Jewish exile to Babylon. The Buddha, Siddhartha Gautama, was not a god or a prophet. He was a man who understood life in the deepest way possible, which is to say that he became enlightened. He decided to teach others to grow toward enlightenment. His teachings (the Dharma) have withstood the test of time. It is a philosophy and a way of life to those who learn that wealth does not guarantee happiness."

"It began in northern India, correct?" Stuart asked.

"Yes, in what today is southern Nepal," the monk replied. "There are many different types of Buddhism, just as there are many different types of Protestant churches. There are territorial differences and differences in customs and cultures. What does not change is the teaching—the Dharma or truth."

"Can you summarize up what the Dharma is?" Stuart asked.

The monk smiled, "The core of Buddhist teachings are the Four

Noble Truths and The Noble Eightfold Path." He held up a finger as he recited each truth. "Life has inevitable suffering. There is a cause to our suffering. There is an end to our suffering. The end to suffering is contained in the Eightfold Path."

"Why is it called Noble?" Jennifer asked.

"At that time the word *noble* implied royalty," the monk answered. "The highest or most revered would be another way to describe it. Buddha wanted these teachings to be understood in the fullest and that nothing else could be more important to any one individual."

Stuart interjected, "In chemistry, noble metals do not combine readily with other metals, meaning they are pure."

Jennifer gave Stuart a questioning look. The monk smiled, nodded his head, and said, "That is right; however, this form of chemistry wasn't around during the time of the Buddha. But you can interpret the words *Noble Truths* to be pure truths or highest truths."

"It seems pretty easy to understand that part of life is suffering," Stuart said.

"It is much more than just suffering or unhappiness," the monk replied. In Sanskrit, the word *dukkha* means unsatisfying or incomplete. Think of it as a wheel in which the axle is off center. A person will have a bumpy ride of life unless he can center it. Because of the way humans live their lives, they are always going to be dissatisfied."

"So if the cause of dissatisfaction can be found and removed as the other Noble Truths imply, then humans can live satisfied? Is that what you're saying?" Jennifer asked.

"I'm not talking about being comfortable or having things that make us happy," the monk replied. "I'm talking about satisfaction in the sense that it is unconditional. Humans are addicted to a world that simply cannot provide lasting satisfaction, in this modern culture more than ever. The word Buddha uses for the cause of this dissatisfaction is *tanha*, which means unquenchable thirst.

Engaging in the stuff of life—romance, labor, finance, etc.—may be satisfactory for a while, but it is never completely satisfying. It may even become a burden. The great insight of Buddha was that the problem was not the world or the stuff of life but the addiction itself. It isn't what we are wanting or craving but that we want in the first place that causes dissatisfaction."

"So again, if we remove the cause of dissatisfaction or wanting, we can be satisfied?" Jennifer asked again.

"Yes," the monk replied. "The word in Sanskrit for cessation of suffering is *nirvana*, the third Noble Truth. It also means to extinguish the craving or wanting. Nirvana isn't a state of mind or a feeling. It is beyond all of that and any condition at all, whether mental, physical, emotional, or spiritual. You can be sad or hungry and still be satisfied in the deepest sense. You see, when we believe that people or things are the source of our satisfaction, we are in trouble when they no longer exist. The fourth Noble Truth is the path to extinguish the wanting. It is called *marga* in Sanskrit.

"It is my guess that the Eightfold Path is a little bit harder to understand or follow," Stuart remarked.

The monk smiled again. Again, he held up fingers as he recited the Eightfold Path. "Right understanding, right thinking, right speech, right conduct, right livelihood, right effort, right mindfulness, and right concentration. To put it simply, it is to be moral in what we say or do. Meditation helps us focus our minds on being fully aware of our thoughts and actions. By understanding the Four Noble Truths, we gain wisdom. The path requires courage, patience, flexibility, and intelligence."

"Does Buddhism have a list of dos and don'ts for its followers?" Stuart asked.

"There are many rules of conduct that all Buddhists are supposed to observe, but the Five Precepts summarize them all:

Do not take the life of anything living, do not take anything not freely given, abstain from sexual misconduct, refrain from untrue speech, and avoid intoxication. There are things Buddhists are encouraged to do: sharing compassion, learning wisdom, developing mindfulness, and getting together at celebrations for fellowship in the community."

"One last question," Stuart said as he looked at his watch. "What does the Buddhist believe about life after death?"

"We believe in reincarnation," the monk said. "Human energies and nature have constantly been flowing together forever. The universe is infinite and continues to recreate itself through a repetition of birth and death. After someone dies, there is an in-between time and place to go before rebirth, the afterlife, so to speak. We also believe in karma, the law that good intentions lead to positive outcomes while negative behaviors and intentions ultimately lead to negative outcomes. A person does not return to Earth as the exact same entity again. Our souls are on a continual journey toward the ultimate enlightenment."

"Thank you," Stuart said as he rose to shake the monk's hand. "You have given me a lot to think about."

"It was nice meeting you," Jennifer said. As they were walking toward the exit, she asked, "Do you meet on Sundays?"

"Yes," the monk replied. "We also have Tuesday evening services and Friday meditations. There is always something going on here at the temple, whether it be social gatherings, educational opportunities, or service projects. Anyone is welcome."

"Goodbye," Jennifer and Stuart said in unison as they exited the temple.

"*Anjali Mudra,*" the Venerable Sarada said as he bowed.

As they drove away, Stuart said, "That's a lot to wrap my head around."

"Yeah, it seems like a peaceful religion or practice," Jennifer replied. I'll bet there's never been a Buddhist mass murderer."

"Well, if there were, the bad karma would take care of it in the next life," Stuart said, smiling. "Do you want to go to dinner … and maybe a movie afterward?"

"What kind of movie?" Jennifer asked warily. "I don't do horror or war."

"I think there is a new *Mission Impossible* out," Stuart said, eyeing her sideways.

"Ooooh, Tom Cruise. Sure thing," Jennifer said, laughing at his attempt at eye rolling.

NINE

Buddhism: The Way to Enlightenment

Stuart Jones, Editor
(For publication Saturday, August 13)

All that we are is the result of what we have thought. The mind is everything. What we think we become. Sometimes it is better to be kind than to be right. We do not need an intelligent mind that speaks, but a patient heart that listens. You will not be punished for your anger. You will be punished by your anger.

—Buddha

Siddhartha Gautama, otherwise known as the Buddha, was born into a royal family on the northern edge of the Ganges River Basin in an area today known as southern Nepal. He was born sometime between the sixth and fourth centuries BC. According to legend, he had a privileged childhood. But upon seeing suffering in the world outside the palace, he resolved to renounce his wealth and family and live the traditional life of a wandering holy man or seeker of truth.

The word *Buddha* means one who is awake in Sanskrit. Buddha became very skilled in meditation and transforming his mind to achieve freedom from suffering or wanting; otherwise known as becoming enlightened. He spread his understanding of the Four Noble Truths around northeast India and established orders for monks and nuns. This religion and philosophy spread to Central and Southeast Asia, China, Korea, and Japan.

Buddhism plays a central role in the spiritual and social life of Asia. In the beginning of the twentieth century, it spread westward. Today in a Buddhist temple, anyone can develop a deep understanding of the Four Noble Truths: Life has inevitable suffering, there is a cause to our suffering, there is an end to our suffering, and the end to suffering is contained in the Eightfold Path. The Eightfold Path serves as instructions for leading a moral life and learning to be happy with what you have. Wanting things or having things are okay as long as they are not regarded as a source of satisfaction in life. Meditation is a key part of the Buddhist's life. With meditation and mindfulness and as one lives the precepts of the path, one hopes to achieve nirvana or enlightenment.

Buddhists believe in reincarnation and in the law of karma (actions have results). This explains inequality in the world, why some have shorter lives than others, and why some have afflictions. Karma emphasizes the importance of all individuals being responsible for their actions, past and present. Karmic deeds, either good or bad, will bear fruit in this life or in future lives. The relationship between existences in rebirth is explained by the analogy of fire, which maintains itself unchanged in appearance, and yet it is different in every moment. The soul is on a continual journey toward various levels of enlightenment.

Buddhism explains the purpose to life and provides a code of practice or way of life that leads to happiness, whether you are rich or poor, sick or healthy, or mournful or elated. There are Five

Precepts all Buddhists must follow: Do not take the life of anything living, do not take anything not freely given, abstain from sexual misconduct and overindulgence, refrain from untrue speech, and avoid intoxication or the absence of mindfulness.

There are various communities of Buddhists in temples around the world, which have developed culturally. But all have the same Four Noble Truths, the Eightfold Path, and the Five Precepts for their followers. Here in the greater metro area, there are nearly eighty temples, monasteries, or gathering places for Buddhists. Nearly every day, there are meetings, educational programs, instruction for meditation, and social gatherings. Those who seek their own path to enlightenment are welcome.

TEN

The Journey

"Hey, Jo Jo. What's up?" Stuart answered his phone while descending the subway stairs. "Are you and Big Dan still overseas?" he continued.

"Stuart!" Jo Jo shouted into the phone. "It's noisy here, so I have to shout. I'm standing in the middle of a runway to scramble the call. We've been getting a lot of chatter, and the boss wants you to come here to visit our favorite imam."

"I don't think I can Jo Jo. I just started my job," Stuart replied.

"I know. Perfect cover, right?" Jo Jo interrupted. "The colonel told me to tell you to come to the source. It is nearly the end of the hajj. The chatter is centered in Mecca. If your editor won't pay, we can get our source on it."

"Maybe I can ask to use embed funds. I know they have a couple of reporters in Afghanistan," Stuart thought aloud. "Let me run it by my editor, I might be able to make it work. Can I bring my assistant?"

"Only if she's hot," Jo Jo countered.

"How do you know she is a she?" Stuart laughed.

"I can hear the smile in your voice, which is kind of a nice change," Jo Jo said.

"Yeah, well she has taken my mind off of the past," Stuart agreed.

"Tell me what time to expect you for tea," Jo Jo said before hanging up. Stuart exited the turnstile and turned up the avenue to *The Times* office.

"Good morning, Mrs. B., Jennifer," Stuart said as he swept by Mrs. B.'s desk where they were looking at her computer.

"My, you sound sunny today," Jennifer smiled.

"Do you think your father would pay for us to go to Saudi Arabia to interview an imam? It is nearing the end of the hajj, and we can interview the pilgrims," Stuart said.

"Are women allowed to go?" Jennifer asked in return.

"Well, we wouldn't be allowed in the mosque, and it might be a problem traveling together since we aren't married or related, but surely with our journalism credentials, we could make it work," Stuart replied a bit hesitantly.

"My nephew can make you look like an Arab man, Jennifer," Mrs. B. piped in. "He does makeup for the university's theater productions. We can get you a robe like they wear and a headscarf."

"It is called a thobe," Stuart added. "I wouldn't need to wear one. Because I will be clearly westernized, I will be the one standing out, not you. The pilgrims will be concentrating on their spiritual journey. There are usually a ton of journalists hanging around taking pictures and the like."

"Won't the imam object to my being there if he suspects I am not really a man?" Jennifer asked.

"You won't get that close. I have a couple of other contacts that will be part of our group. You can just smile and take lots of pictures. Hopefully, it will be a sunny day, and you can wear sunglasses," Stuart replied.

"I hope my passport isn't out of date," Jennifer remarked. "I'll check it as soon as I get home today. Then tomorrow, I'll make arrangements for flights."

"We better clear it with your dad first," Stuart suggested. "When can we meet your nephew Mrs. B.?" Stuart asked.

"Why don't you come over for dinner tomorrow night," she replied. "I'll have him bring all the stuff he'll need for the makeover. He is very good at explaining exactly what to do."

Two days later, they were seated in the rear of a Saudi Airlines jumbo jet. "I can't believe we are actually going to Mecca," Jennifer said. "You mentioned that you knew this imam from when you were in the Middle East previously. Was that when you were a soldier?"

"Well, yes and no," Stuart answered. "He is a relative of someone I knew in high school. We have worked together on some U.S.-Saudi training sessions."

Jennifer thought he sounded purposefully vague, but she was tired and did not want to press the issue. *If he wants me to know about his past, he will tell me,* she thought. She shut off the light above her head and settled down in her seat to try to get some sleep. She had a sense of foreboding when she thought about her plan to dress as a man in an Arab culture. But even she hadn't recognized herself once Mrs. B.'s nephew was done with her. She told herself, *You are just tired. Tomorrow is going to be an exciting day.*

ELEVEN

The Imam

"I thought you said your assistant was a female," Jo Jo stated in surprise when he approached Stuart with a small Saudi-looking man.

Stuart grinned and said, "Jo Jo, this is Jennifer, aka James, the photographer. Jennifer, meet Jo Jo."

"No way!" Jo Jo exclaimed. "You had me fooled. Very good makeup artist."

"As long as she doesn't talk," Stuart said as he smiled at Jennifer. "Is Big Dan bringing the wires?"

"Wires?" Jennifer inquired.

"I see what you mean about talking," Jo Jo concurred. "There are tens of thousands of people where we are going. We want to be wired up to hear each other," Jo Jo said, "and also have a bead on everyone's location in case we get separated. Mike will be in the van monitoring the situation."

Once they had their earpieces in place, they filed out of the hotel in Jeddah and into the waiting van. Stuart cautioned her not to speak unless it was absolutely necessary. He would be speaking with the imam in Arabic. The others could listen in. "You should take as many pictures as you can," Stuart told her. "Even though we won't be able to enter the actual city, there is a nice museum on the outskirts with a great view of the city and the Great Mosque. A replica of the Great Mosque is outside the museum where we will meet the imam. Try to stay in eye contact with each other."

Stuart made some sort of head gesture toward her as he eyed Jo Jo and Dan. They nodded in return. Something about their movements made Jennifer think this was not simply a talk with the imam. She suddenly felt very aware of their attention on her. She tried to act casual as she adjusted the knobs and lens of her camera. The van came to a stop, and they filed out. The sight was awe-inspiring. The sprawled-out city was nestled in the barren hills. In the center was a circular field surrounding a huge structure. In the middle of the field, there was a black cube.

Stuart came up beside her and said, "It's the largest mosque in the world. According to Islamic tradition, it was first constructed by angels. I'm sorry we can't get any closer, but only Muslims are allowed in the city. Do you see the black cube in the center? It is the Holy Kaaba. According to the Holy Qur'an, it was built by Abraham and his son Ishmael. Millions of pilgrims travel here to participate in the Umrah to fulfill the fifth Pillar of Islam. I don't think you can see it from here, but there is a spring called the Zamzam well. Allah provided it to Hagar to save Ismael's life."

"Oh, wow," Jennifer said and started taking pictures. She was glad she had brought the larger lens. She turned around when she heard Stuart talking in her ear.

"*As-salamu Alaikum*," Stuart said as he bowed to Imam Musa. They were speaking Arabic, and they seemed to be rather familiar with each other. She glanced over at Jo Jo and Dan, who were standing together and looking in opposite directions. She got the feeling they were staring at her through their sunglasses. She turned around and continued taking pictures while the Arabic conversation was going on in her ear. After about fifteen minutes, she headed over to Dan and gave him her camera.

"I have to go to the bathroom," she mouthed to him, not wanting to throw off Stuart in his conversation.

"Remember to go to the men's," Dan whispered back to her. She nodded and headed across the courtyard to the side building where universal bathroom signs were posted. They were identified in about ten different languages, but she could tell which one was for men. Luckily, it was empty, and she headed for the single stall. Just as she flushed, she heard the door open. She decided to skip handwashing and planned to make a quick exit out the door. There were three men standing in front of the door. One of them grabbed her and shoved her against the wall.

"What are you doing?" she shrieked. The second man flashed a knife and shouted at her in Arabic. They grabbed her arms and practically carried her out the door. They made a sharp left turn through an unmarked door. It must have locked as it shut because she could hear pounding on the door as they dragged her through the hall to the exit.

"Jennifer," she heard Dan shout in her earpiece, "what happened?"

"Help me!" Jennifer cried out. "They put me in a van." The van peeled away from the curb. The man wielding the knife held it up to her face and shouted at her in Arabic. She was certain that he was telling her to shut up.

"Jennifer," Stuart said in her ear. "Don't talk, just listen. I want you to cough to let me know how many men took you." Jennifer coughed three times as she looked into the angry eyes of her attacker.

"Okay, that's good. We are getting into our van right now. We have a bead on your location. We will be right behind you. Don't talk. Remain calm. I won't let them hurt you," Stuart told her in a low voice. "Hurry up, Jo Jo!" she heard Stuart shouting in her ear. She hoped the attackers would not be able to hear him. The van was swerving, turning, and tossing her from side to side. Eventually, it came to an abrupt stop. The attacker with the knife held it up to her throat, then removed it, and motioned for her to get out of the van. The other two came up behind her, grabbed her arms, and dragged her into a house through a side door. It was so quick she couldn't see if she was still in the town or not. They pushed her into the room, and she fell to the ground unable to get her feet under her. She looked up at three angry Arab-looking men dressed in western clothing. One sat down at the table and pulled out his phone. He started to take a picture of her, but the one with the knife stopped him and headed over to her. He reached down and grabbed her headdress. The headdress came off, and her long locks fell down her shoulders.

"Stuart, they know I am not a man," Jennifer said quietly as her terror grew with each spoken word.

"Jennifer, we're coming," Stuart said quietly, but she could tell he was trying to remain calm. The attackers pulled her up to her feet and held her arms while the man with the knife slit up the center of her garb. He ripped her T-shirt and panties. Then he grabbed the beard and yanked on it hard, but it was glued too tightly, so her head was yanked to the side. She was glad the wire ran down her back because they hadn't discovered it yet. She looked into the eyes of her attackers and saw anger and lust. They dragged her to the table and slammed her down hard on the surface. The knife once again was placed at her throat, and two attackers held her down shouting instructions to the third.

"They are going to rape me!" Jennifer shouted as she lost all semblance of quiet and calm. The third attacker pulled down his pants and moved over her. As she felt the knife starting to cut into her skin, her body froze in place.

"We're here. Stay down!" barked a voice she didn't recognize. All she could see was the huge penis of her attacker coming toward her. Then he fell on her. She felt a hot sticky substance run down the inside of her thigh. At the same time, the knife fell away from her neck, and the arms holding her down were gone. Stuart pulled her up to him and held her tightly in his arms, shielding her nakedness from the others.

"Jennifer, I'm so sorry," Stuart whispered in her ear. "I'm so sorry."

Jo Jo spoke up. "Captain, look." Everyone turned to the sound of his voice and saw that he was standing in a doorway that led into a room filled with computers.

"Pay dirt," the stranger said. "Clear it out. Ten minutes tops. Jo Jo, start the gas."

The man known as the captain handed Stuart two blankets, which turned out to be burkas. "Put these on!" he barked. "Take her two blocks east. Dan will pick you up in the other van. Be at the airfield in thirty minutes. The plane is on its way. It must be loaded and wheels up in forty minutes. Stuart was helping her into a tunnel of darkness. She could barely stand or see. He put on the other burka and then supported her as they hobbled out the front door.

"Jennifer, you have to walk," Stuart told her as he grabbed her hand and pulled her along beside him. They looked like two old women hunched over with their heads together. He tried to go as fast as possible without rousing too much suspicion from passing motorists. Luckily, there weren't any. Just as they reached the second curb, a van pulled over in front of them.

"Get in," Stuart ordered. "Dan, we need to go to the hotel first to get our passports and bags." He peeled off the burka but left Jennifer in hers.

"I don't think we'll make the airfield," Dan replied looking back at the burka-clad person beside Stuart. He raised his eyebrows.

"I know a back way. Just drive," barked Stuart as Dan peeled away from the curb. The sound of an explosion rocked the vehicle slightly as it sped away toward the hotel. Jennifer looked around and saw flames leaping out from what used to be her captor's house. She turned to look at Stuart, but he was looking sternly out the front window. His jaw was clenched in a grimace. "Pull up in front," barked Stuart.

"I can't park here," Dan complained.

"I'll just be a minute," Stuart countered. "I don't see security."

Jennifer watched as he took the steps two at a time and disappeared into the hotel. She was beginning to shake. She couldn't stop herself.

"Shit!" Dan exclaimed as he looked into the rearview mirror. "Don't say a word," he told her. He got out of the car, went around to the front tires, and looked at them like there might be a problem. She turned around, looked out the back window, and saw two security guards with guns sauntering in their direction. He looked up, nodded toward the men, and then came around to the driver's door.

"We gotta go," he said. Just as he signaled to pull out into the road, the back passenger door flew open. Stuart jumped in, barely shutting the door before the guards reached the side of the van.

"Head west at the next intersection. We'll take the cart path around the town to the airfield," Stuart commanded. "Let's get a move on it!"

"What the hell happened?" Dan asked, looking into the rearview mirror.

"Not now," Stuart said, firmly meeting his gaze in the mirror.

Stuart felt Jennifer shaking uncontrollably and put his arms around her. "Jenny, hold on. We'll be there soon. I have your bag. You can get out of this when we get on the plane," Stuart said, making reference to her burka.

"I'm sorry. I can't stop shaking," Jennifer said feebly.

"You're in shock," Stuart told her. "Here, lie down and put your head in my lap."

"I think I'm going to be sick," Jennifer replied.

"Just concentrate on your breathing," Stuart told her gently. "Look at me. Breathe in through your nose. Slowly, slowly. Now out through your mouth." She could just make out his face through the dark opening in the veil. He looked worried. She squeezed his hand, trying to reassure him. He looked down at her and smiled.

"Do you have any money?" Dan asked. "Are we going to have to bribe a guard?"

Stuart reached into his pocket and pulled out a wad of riyal. "Here," he said, handing them to Dan. They could see the huge C-130 coming in for a landing as they turned into the cargo area.

"You talk," Dan said, looking at him in the rearview mirror. "Your Arabic is better than mine."

Stuart let go of Jennifer and climbed into the passenger seat. "Cover yourself up Jennifer," he said. "And start praying."

When the van pulled slowly up to the gate, a guard stared at them through the window of the guardhouse. He sauntered slowly toward the driver's door and demanded in Arabic, "Let me see your papers."

Stuart leaned over and calmly spoke. "We were supposed to meet another van here, but we were stuck in traffic. They have our papers. Didn't they give them to you?" Dan handed the guard the money, and Stuart said, "Will these papers do?"

The guard looked down at the wad of cash in his hand and slowly turned to open the gate as he pocketed the money. Dan drove to the center of the airfield and pulled into the back of the C-130 just behind the other van. The plane was taxiing even before the rear cargo door began to close.

Dan jumped out of the van and said, "You stay here with her. I can get this tied down."

"Dan," Stuart called after him. "Bring me some water. She's in shock."

TWELVE

The Confession

Stuart sat behind Jennifer and helped her take off the burka, her torn clothing, and the wire. She was still shaking, so he had to fasten her bra for her and guide her arms into her shirt. He moved around to the front and looked straight into her eyes while he buttoned her shirt. She waved off the spare panties and grabbed her jeans. He guided in one leg at a time and helped her pull them up while she lay down. He covered her with the burka and helped her drink a little warm water. She struggled to sit up as she asked him, "Did you get the bottle of acetone?"

"If it was in the bag, I did," he replied. "Here," he said, pulling it out of her bag. She began to rub the beard with an acetone-soaked edge of her torn T-shirt. The beard began to peel away slowly. Her chin and cheeks were rubbed red and raw when she finally got it peeled away.

"Hand me that Vaseline," she said as she put the cap back on the acetone. He opened the jar and rubbed the petroleum jelly on her chin and cheeks. "This wasn't just about interviewing an imam, was it?" she asked Stuart while looking him directly in the eyes.

"Yes and no," Stuart replied, looking down at the jar of Vaseline.

"What the hell happened?" she asked. "Who was the imam? You knew him. I could tell by the way you were conversing. Why do you know so much about Islam?" Her questions rolled out of her mouth so fast that he didn't have time to answer. He put the jar back in her bag, sat down, and pulled her over to sit beside him. Their backs were against the van's wall. He put his arm around her, held her against his chest, and stroked her hair with his free hand. He could feel her shaking still and could hear her weak sniffles.

"Jennifer," he said quietly and slowly, "this wasn't supposed to happen. We were just going to talk to Imam Musa because he was supposed to have information on an al-Qaeda cell. You do know that what happened to you has nothing to do with Islam, don't you? Islam is a peaceful religion. Those terrorists are just like the ecoterrorists and right-wing nut jobs who bomb abortion clinics."

"How do you know the imam?" she asked.

"It's a long story," he said softly.

She looked at him for a long while as he continued to stare out the window of the van. "How long does it take to get where we are going, and where are we going?" she asked with a little anger creeping into her tone.

He replied with resignation in his voice, "Ramstein Air Base in Germany. It will take about six hours. Here, lie down and put your head in my lap. Put your feet up on the window ledge, so you can get some color back in your cheeks."

After a while she said, "Well?"

"I'm trying to figure out where to begin," he answered.

"Begin at the beginning," she demanded.

"It really begins with my earliest memories," he told her as he stretched out his legs. "My mom had me when she was very young. I never knew who my father was. We lived in a small house with her friend from high school. They worked a lot. Sometimes my mom had three jobs just to make ends meet. I stayed with a family who lived next door. They had a son my age, and his mother stayed home. They were Muslim. I practically grew up in their family. Their son, Samil, became my best friend. He was a brother, really. We did everything together: sports, clubs, religious services. I started to read the Qur'an when I was six. When I was seventeen, I went with his family to Mecca for the hajj."

"No wonder you know so much about it," Jennifer interjected. "Where is Samil now?"

Stuart stared out the window of the van. He was silent for so long that she wondered if he had heard her. Something about his silence was foreboding. He had a sadness about his face that looked so lonely. She waited. "After 9/11 we joined the Army," he finally continued. "Imam Musa from our mosque joined with us. When the higher-ups realized that we were fluent in Arabic, they asked us if we wanted to join Special Forces, and we did. We spent three years in Afghanistan. On the day before we were to come home, Sam stepped on a land mine. I was about a hundred yards away, and I heard the click. We looked at each other just before it blew."

Stuart was struggling to breathe. A tear was slipping down his cheek. "I held the upper half of his body in my arms while it took a few minutes for him to die. He told me that he loved me and to tell his parents that he loved them." Stuart was holding his head in his hands and trying not to sob. Jennifer pulled him gently down beside her so that she could wrap her arms around him. "I just don't believe in anything anymore," he whispered.

"I'm so sorry, Stuart," she said, not knowing what else to say. They fell asleep in each other's arms to the sound of the airplane's motor and the jostling of the van tied into the holding bay. Jennifer woke after a fitful sleep. She had her back to Stuart, and his arms were around her. She thought that they fit together well. Then she sensed a growing knot at her back. She froze.

"I would never hurt you, Jennifer," Stuart whispered. "I wouldn't be much of a man if I wasn't aroused while holding a beautiful woman in my arms." He released her and sat up. "I'm sorry if it scared you, but I'm not sorry you have that effect on me. She sat up and gave him a half smile. They gazed into each other's eyes until she looked away, only to grow a full smile.

THIRTEEN

The Debriefing

"General," Stuart snapped a salute as the heavily decorated soldier walked through the door of the office.

"At ease, Jones," he replied, all the while looking at Jennifer. "Ms. Carter, I presume?"

"Hello, General," Jennifer said as she reached out to shake his hand.

He looked at it and proceeded to position himself behind his desk. "Let's be seated, shall we?" he said as he gestured to the two guest chairs. "I want to hear what happened in Jeddah." He looked at Stuart. The next thirty minutes were spent rehashing the terrible ordeal. Jennifer was too scared to say anything. She could feel herself nodding at times and holding her breath on more than one occasion.

"You need to take her to the clinic to get that cut on her neck looked at," General Jackson ordered. "Get a DNA test, too, if you get my drift," he added. Jennifer looked at Stuart questioningly, but he simply put his hand on hers and kept looking at the general. General Jackson stood and began pacing behind his desk. "What I am about to tell you is top secret. It could jeopardize the operation if any news were leaked. Do I make myself clear?" he asked Stuart and Jennifer, who could only nod. He continued, "The computers recovered in the al-Qaeda cell house unveiled valuable information on the whereabouts of Osama Bin Laden. As we speak, there is a team traveling to locate him and take him out. I only share this with you Ms. Carter because you very damn near gave your life for your country, and I believe I can trust you." Jennifer was shocked. All she could do was nod her head. "Dismissed!" General Jackson barked as he made his way out of the office through the door behind his desk.

Stuart scrambled to his feet to salute, but the general had already shut the door. "Come on," he told her. "Let's get you to the clinic. We have about four hours before our plane leaves for Frankfurt."

"Oooouch!" Jennifer squealed as a medic scraped the dried blood away from her neck.

"Sorry, miss," he said. "We need to clean this out properly, and it looks like you will need a couple of sutures. It's a good thing he missed your carotid artery. He might have nicked your jugular though. It's a good thing you clot well." Jennifer rolled her eyes and then glanced toward the knocking sound at the door.

A female in a lab coat walked into the room. "Hello, I'm Doctor Addy," she said pleasantly. "Did you order a rape kit?"

"Stuart?" Jennifer said with uncertainty.

"Jennifer," he said calmly to her. "We need to see if we can identify the DNA your attacker left."

"Oh," Jennifer whispered.

"I'll be very gentle," Dr. Addy said as she smiled. "Unfortunately, I have had too much practice at this. I was at New York General during my residency." Dr. Addy covered Jennifer with a warm sheet. Jennifer could feel her warm hands gripping her ankles while she placed her feet in stirrups and bent her knees. She unfolded a kit wrapped in sterile paper and began assembling instruments and vials on the stand next to her. "You will feel a little pressure. Just breathe through it." Dr. Addy assured her as she placed an instrument in her vagina. "Oh! Your hymen is largely intact," Dr. Addy exclaimed as she withdrew the instrument. "I thought this was a rape?" she said as she looked questioningly at Stuart.

"It was attempted rape," Stuart replied. "The attacker ejaculated on her. We were hoping to retrieve some of the attacker's DNA."

"I see," the doctor said. "Let me get the UV light and have a look." She stood up and walked over to a cabinet across the room.

Jennifer winced as the medic injected lidocaine into the wound at her neck. "Sorry, miss, but you will be happier with it numb as I place the sutures," he told her.

Dr. Addy returned and moved the table around to the end of the bed so that Jennifer could not see what she was doing. "There is definitely some fluid here on the inside upper right thigh and crotch area."

"Yes," Jennifer spoke up. "That is where I felt a warm sticky fluid right before he collapsed on me."

"Did he have a heart attack?" Dr. Addy queried.

"That's classified," Stuart said. "Just try to get enough to run a DNA analysis."

"I can't be sure there isn't some vaginal fluid here," Dr. Addy remarked.

"If there are multiple DNA sequences, we can cross that bridge when the time comes. Just collect it and send it to the lab," Stuart ordered.

They were out of breath after the full-on run toward the Lufthansa gate in Frankfurt. They made it with a few minutes to spare. "I need to use the bathroom," Jennifer told Stuart.

"Okay, hurry. We are boarding soon," Stuart replied. He walked to the desk and inquired whether they could upgrade to first class.

"That will be €938," the desk attendant replied. "You are lucky to get the last two adjacent seats."

"Thanks," Stuart replied. He was glad to be able to surprise Jennifer even though it would make the rest of the month a little tight. *Good thing I like macaroni and cheese,* he thought. The announcement came to begin the boarding process for their flight. Stuart looked around for Jennifer. Fear gripped his chest, and he began to breathe more rapidly. He was frantically looking up and down the airport mall when he spotted her ponytail bouncing behind a soccer team. He ran toward her and pulled her into his arms.

"What?" she asked.

"I was panicking and remembering the last time you went to the bathroom by yourself," Stuart whispered while continuing to hold her tightly.

"Stuart," she said pushing herself back. "I hope this won't happen every time I go to the bathroom. This one was closed for cleaning, and I had to go back to the entrance to find an open one."

"Oh," he said meekly, feeling a little foolish but greatly relieved. "Come on. Let's board."

"They are only boarding first class," she remarked.

"I know," Stuart said, smiling. "I got us upgraded."

"Oh, wow!" Jennifer replied. "I've never been in first class before."

They settled into their seats. The attendant brought them a glass of champagne, which they gladly accepted. "Cheers," Jennifer said and clinked glasses with Stuart.

"Cheers," Stuart replied. "To the success of the mission."

"Yes, to the success," Jennifer chimed in. She quieted and noticed all the people filing down the aisle. The silence between them was comfortable. She looked out the window at the hubbub of the ground crew.

"Ladies and gentlemen," began the steward as he went through the preflight announcements.

She felt the plane push back from the gate. Sleep was calling to her. She sighed and turned her body to look at Stuart full on. She was very serious as she said, "You know, Stuart, I think that there was divine providence in this whole trip. I know you said you don't believe in God anymore, but I can't help but believe he had a hand in the way this whole trip unfolded, almost as if it was planned. I feel that God has been with us the entire way." She couldn't get a read on his vacant expression. "I wonder how the mission is going," she said after a while.

He smiled at her and said, "I'm glad I told you about Sammi. It doesn't hurt quite so much now that I talked about it, and someone else knows."

"Would you like me to go with you to see his parents?" she asked.

"Let me think about it," he replied. "The last couple of days have given me a lot to process." He turned away and saw that they had taxied and that they were now ready for takeoff. He downed the rest of the champagne and shut his eyes. He didn't wake up when Jennifer relieved him of his glass and reclined his seat.

"Daddy!" Jennifer exclaimed as she opened her apartment door. She and Stuart entered the foyer and looked at the concerned face of Henry Carter.

"You're a day late, and you didn't call. You weren't on your return flight from Saudi Arabia," Henry barked.

"That's because we came back through Germany," Jennifer

responded. "I'm sorry. I should have left a message, but we have literally been on plane after plane. I really didn't have a chance."

"Why did you come back through Germany?" Henry asked.

"It's a long story," Jennifer answered as she reached her father to give him a kiss on the cheek.

Henry looked over her shoulder, said, "Stuart," and nodded.

"Henry." Stuart acknowledged the nod. "Well, I'll leave you to it." He looked at Jennifer. "See you Monday?"

"Yes, thank you, Stuart." Jennifer smiled at him as he headed toward the door.

"Wait!" Henry called after him. "Did you hear they got Bin Laden?"

Stuart turned back. Instead of looking at Henry, he looked at Jennifer. The spark of understanding that went between them was almost palpable. "Yes, we saw it on CNN at the airport."

"I put Jensen on the story," Henry said. "He was our imbed during Operation Enduring Freedom."

"I'll leave you now," Stuart said while smiling at Jennifer and going out the door.

"What aren't you telling me, Jennifer?" Henry asked his daughter.

Jennifer reddened. "You could always read my mind, Dad. Come on. Let's go to the deli and get some supper. I'll tell you all about it."

Henry was red-faced and gripping his utensils so forcefully that he was bending them. "I can't believe that bastard nearly got you killed!" he hissed.

"Dad," Jennifer hissed back. "He saved my life!" Henry was so flabbergasted that he couldn't think. "Dad," Jennifer said more softly while reaching out to loosen his hand from the fork, "the information they found at the house is what enabled them to find Bin Laden."

Henry stared at her with his mouth agape. "So, it was a military mission?" he asked incredulously. "He took you on a military mission?"

"No, it wasn't meant to be that. We were just going to talk to his friend, the imam he knew from childhood, get pictures of Mecca, and interview pilgrims," Jennifer reassured him. "I really can't explain the coincidence, other than divine intervention. I'm not hurt. I really care about him, Dad."

"I can't lose you too, Jenny," Henry said while holding her hand.

"You aren't going to lose me, Dad," Jennifer said. "You might gain a son-in-law, but you'll never lose your daughter."

"Is it that serious?" Henry asked.

"I don't know," Jennifer said. "I only know that I've never felt this way before. It might be hero complex, but I think we are enough alike to be boring like you and Mom and different enough to be spicy."

Henry raised his eyebrow at that last remark and said, "Your mother and I were never boring."

"Promise me you are not going to berate him for what happened," Jennifer demanded.

Henry looked into the eyes of his daughter and knew that he would never want to be a disappointment in them. They looked too much like Naomi's. "I promise," he conceded.

"Let's go to church tomorrow," Jennifer suggested. "It is time. We've been away for long enough."

Henry smiled and squeezed her hand. "You're right."

FOURTEEN

Islam: Descendants of Abraham through Ishmael

Stuart Jones, Editor
(To be published Saturday, September 10, 2011)

Our Lord, I have settled some of my offspring in a valley of no vegetation, by Your Sacred House, our Lord, so that they may perform the prayers. So make the hearts of some people incline towards them, and provide them with fruits, that they may be thankful."

—Qur'an 14:37

Say, "We believe in Allah, and in what was revealed to us; and in what was revealed to Abraham, and Ishmael, and Isaac, and Jacob, and the Patriarchs; and in what was given to Moses, and Jesus, and the prophets from their Lord. We make no distinction between any of them, and to Him we submit."

—Qur'an 3:84

> The people most deserving of Abraham are those
> who followed him, and this prophet (Muhammad),
> and those who believe. God is the Guardian of the
> believers.
>
> —Qur'an 3:68

Islam is a monotheistic religion, which descended from Abraham through his son Ishmael. Abraham was called to sacrifice Ishmael, who was willing to comply. But his faith saved Ishmael, and Allah blessed them with descendants as numerous as the stars. They built a house of worship in Mecca (Holy Kaaba) on a site once thought to have been visited by angels. The white cornerstone was provided by the angel Gabriel, who through time and the introduction of idol worship in the area, turned black. At the age of forty, the prophet Muhammad received a message from the angel Gabriel to write the Qur'an, the final revelation of God, in order to make the people, once again, believe in the one and true God. Over a period of twenty-three years, he received revelations and taught them to his companions and followers, some of whom were tasked with writing them down. The Qur'an was written on many different materials, such as animal bones and pieces of hide. At the time of Muhammad's death, the Qur'an had reached a book of six hundred pages. Within two years of his death, the entire work was compiled into one text, which was agreed upon by his followers to be authentic and reliable. Memorization by his followers remains a primary mode of transmission even today.

The family lineage from Ishmael to Muhammad, over forty generations, has been a subject of debate amongst scholars. Muhammad lived from 570 and 632 AD. Followers of Islam believe that he was the ultimate prophet of God. The revelation that there is no other God but God was shared by Muhammad throughout

Mecca and was spread throughout the Middle East, Asia, Europe, Africa, and the West. Islam is the second largest religion in the world and the fastest growing.

The starting point in describing Islam begins with the meaning of the word itself. It means peace through submission. Islam is a way of life in which you find peace as a result of submission to God. The Six Articles of Faith or beliefs that all Muslims believe are the following:

1. They believe in God, who is an all-knowing, all-seeing, and absolute being, with no partners or sons. He is the creator of the universe.
2. They believe in the existence of angels, who are made by God and are made of light. We are unable to perceive these beings, and they exist beyond what is seen. Humans cannot become angels. Satan was not a fallen angel. God tells them what to do.
3. They believe in messengers and prophets who were sent by God—Adam, Noah, Abraham, Ishmael, Isaac, Jacob, Moses, David, and Jesus—all with the purpose of helping others to believe in one God and to do good deeds. There are possibly more than one hundred thousand messengers who have been sent by God to humankind.
4. They believe that some of the messengers received revelations. Moses received the Torah, David received the Psalms, Jesus received the Gospel, and Muhammad received the final scriptures, the Qur'an. The revelations were divine in origin, and the messengers were protected from sin by God. It is worthy to note that the Qur'an was not altered. It is the same revelation that was given to Muhammad by God's angel more than fourteen hundred years ago.
5. They believe in the day of judgment. When we die, God rewards the good and punishes the bad. The good will be

in paradise with God, and the bad will end up in the fires of hell.

6. They believe in God's will and divine decree. God has knowledge of all things that will happen, but he still allows us free will to make choices; thus, we are responsible for our actions.

These beliefs are what make one a Muslim. You might not practice Islam perfectly, and you might make mistakes, but as long as you hold these beliefs, you are considered to be Muslim. The formal acts of worship are known as The Five Pillars of Islam. These are a declaration of faith, prayer, fasting, charity, and pilgrimage. Through proper worship, spiritual development, and purification of the soul, the believer will be led closer to God. The result will be service to humanity.

There are nearly three hundred mosques in the greater metro area. If you wish to reconnect with your faith or explore Islam more thoroughly, you can find a mosque or worship center near you. To practice your faith and serve others as God intended, believe in one God and do good deeds.

FIFTEEN

The Guru

"Morning, Abe, Enid, Mrs. B." Stuart greeted them as he entered the conference room. "Where's Jennifer?"

"Here I am," said a flurry of color as she sped past him and landed in her chair. "I've got Billy Graham!" she exclaimed.

"Well, that's exciting," Mrs. B. chimed in. "How ever did you do that?"

"He's read your articles, Stuart," she said. "He suggested we come to his home in North Carolina next month. It would be fun to take the train, don't you think?"

"Jones!" Henry Carter barked as he looked into the room. "Where's your article on Islam?"

"I ... I just turned it in, Henry," Stuart said as he looked at Jennifer quizzically.

"It's great, Stuart," Abe chimed in. "Very thoughtful."

"How did you read it already?" Stuart asked Abe. "Do you have a pipeline to the server?"

Jennifer cleared her throat and said, "We were just discussing that we got an exclusive with Billy Graham, Dad. I also was able to find a guru to discuss Sikhism with next week."

Enid stood up and put a chart on the whiteboard. "Our sales are up 10 percent," she told the group. "Marketing thinks our section is responsible for at least half of the growth."

Mrs. B. piped in, "We are getting more and more ads from local churches. Jennifer, honey, would you help me lay out a notice board for all the activities they want us to feature?"

"Sure, Mrs. B.," Jennifer replied. "Was there anything else, Dad?"

Henry realized that everyone was looking at him rather strangely after his outburst and said meekly, "No, no, carry on."

"Okay, good work, everyone," Stuart said. Turning to Abe and Enid, he asked, "Are you two okay with my suggestions about fillers? Feel free to add your own."

"We're good," Abe said. "There are plenty of short articles we can write about from your list, right Enid?"

"Do we want to do anything about Bin Laden?" Enid asked.

"Nah, we'll let the newsroom take care of the fallout over his execution," Stuart told her.

Everyone left except Jennifer and Stuart. "Are you okay?" Stuart asked her. "I take it you told your dad what happened."

"He reads me like a book," she said, turning toward the window. "He knew something was up."

"I'm surprised he hasn't fired me," Stuart told her, coming up behind her.

They stood there in comfortable silence looking at the traffic and pedestrians weaving in and out of the busy city street. Slowly, she turned to him and said, "The guru I found is in Middletown."

He looked into her concerned eyes. They were the color of honey with flecks of butter. They crinkled with the sly smile that formed on her face. "How did you know that is where Samil's family lives?" Stuart asked her.

"I'm pretty good with computer searches," she said slyly. "How about I take you to lunch?"

"I could have driven," Stuart told Jennifer once they got on the interstate and headed north.

"I like to drive. Besides, you can write your article on the way back," she reasoned.

"It should only take about three hours," Jennifer said. "Did you remember to bring the recorder?"

Before he could answer her, Stuart's cell phone rang. He pulled it out and said, "Hello?" Jennifer could hear a female voice on the other end, but she couldn't understand what was being said.

"I'm doing great. How are you and Aunt Becky?" Stuart asked. Jennifer heard the muffled female voice again. "Actually, I am on my way to speak to a guru," Stuart responded to the obviously asked question. "No, I'm not driving," he continued. After a few minutes, he said, "That's okay, Mom. You should go with Aunt Becky. You haven't had a vacation in a long time." After another long pause, he said, "To be honest, that really isn't my thing. You will have more fun if it's just you two." He listened again and then said, "All right, next summer then. I'll take you out on the town. Tell Aunt Becky she is invited too. Bye, Mom."

"Well?" Jennifer asked.

"My mother," Stuart answered.

"No, I mean do you have the recorder?" Jennifer asked.

"Oh, yes, I do." Stuart smiled and patted his coat pocket.

After about ten minutes of companionable silence, Jennifer said, "Tell me about your mother."

"Her name is Alice, and she's the hardest working person I know," Stuart began. "She moved in with her sister about five years ago after my uncle died. They live in Lewiston. She has never had just one job. Usually she works two jobs, sometimes three, and she volunteers a lot."

"Sounds like a go-getter," Jennifer remarked.

"To be honest, I have never felt very close to her. I know she had her heart broken when she became pregnant with me and was unable to contact my father. I found out through her best friend that he got drafted. Then his family moved to Canada so that his younger brothers would not get drafted. My grandparents kicked her out. If they ever heard from my father, they never let my mother know. I used to ask her about my father, but because I could see how much it pained her to think about him, I eventually quit asking. We quit communicating all together because both of us really knew that all I wanted to talk about was my dad, so we just quit talking. I did all my talking with Samil's family. She was relieved to have me practically live over there."

"That's so sad, Stuart," Jennifer said. "Did she ever try to find him?"

"Aunt Becky thinks he got married and had a family," Stuart replied. "She doesn't know for sure. It's just from some comments Mom has made. She doesn't even know his name because she was a lot younger than Mom and was a kid when my mom was dating my dad."

"I'm sure she is glad to have you," Jennifer said tenderly. "You are a really good guy."

Stuart smiled at her. "Thanks for thinking that."

"What did she want you to do?" Jennifer asked.

"She and Aunt Becky are going to a spa in California for two weeks over Christmas," he replied. "Not my thing," he said, smiling. "I was planning on staying with her for a few days. To be honest, I am relieved that I don't have to go."

"You can spend Christmas with us!" Jennifer blurted out.

"I don't want to step on your dad's toes," Stuart said.

"Nonsense," Jennifer said, dismissing it. "He likes you, Stuart."

"I don't know; I kind of got the sense he wanted to tear my head off," Stuart responded. "I would probably have had the same reaction if I were him."

"Thank you for meeting with us," Stuart told Mr. Singh as they were ushered into a small conference room near the entrance of the gurdwara, the Sikh place of worship.

"It is my pleasure," Mr. Singh replied. "I was rather surprised to hear from your assistant and about her request. I have since then read your articles on Judaism and Buddhism. I am honored to share Sikhism with your readers."

"So, tell me how Sikhism was founded," Stuart inquired.

"Sikhism was both a monotheistic religion and a philosophy founded by Guru Nanak over five hundred years ago in the Punjab area of India. It is based on meditation and devotion to God. Hearing the divine word through a grace, which was bestowed by God, and having chosen to accept the word, Nanak devoted his life to meditation and ascending to a higher level of peace and joy. Sikhs believe there is a single creator who sustains all people of all faiths." He continued, "For two hundred years, the faith was led by the spirit of God first in Guru Nanak, followed by nine other human gurus. Sikhs believe that all ten gurus were inhabited by the same spirit. Following the death of the tenth guru, Gobind Singh, the spirit of the eternal guru, was transferred to the sacred scripture of Sikhism, Guru Granth Sahib (our holy book), which is now believed to be the sole guru."

"Sikhism is the fifth largest religion in the world with well over twenty-five million followers," Stuart said. "What do all these followers believe?"

Mr. Singh continued. "In Punjabi, Sikh means learner or disciple. Those who join the Sikh community are people who seek spiritual guidance and a connection with God. There is no caste system in Sikhism. All persons are equal and can achieve the peace and joy of being close to God through personal inward meditation. The scripture asks Sikhs to make the best of their time on Earth and to make a connection with God. This includes remembrance of God at all times, living a truthful life, and service to the community."

"What are the religious services like?" Stuart asked.

"It can be quite lively," Mr. Singh responded, smiling. "There are no clergy per se, but there are leaders who are extensively familiar with the scripture called granthis, who lead the singing of scriptures, ceremonies, and celebrations of festivals and offer lectures. The gurdwara," Mr. Singh gestured to the building surrounding them, "is a place for spiritual knowledge. It is also a place of food and shelter for anyone in need. We provide care for the sick, elderly, and handicapped. It is also a place for the moral education of our children. We always have a meal together following services."

"What is required of followers?" Stuart asked.

"Everyone has the sacred duty to make a contribution toward the welfare of humanity—at least 10 percent of our income," Mr. Singh said. "You, of course, notice my clothing falls outside traditional Western fashion." Stuart and Jennifer nodded together. "Unlike other religions where just the clergy are in uniform, we wear an external uniform to remind us of our commitment to the faith. All baptized Sikhs are required to wear the articles of faith, known as the five Ks."

"Does that include a turban for men?" Jennifer asked.

Mr. Singh nodded and smiled, "The Five Articles of Faith in

Punjabi are *kes* (uncut hair), *kanga* (comb), *kara* (a steel bracelet), *kirpan* (a sword), and *kachera* (cotton or soldier's shorts)."

"A sword?" Stuart repeated.

"It can be a small, curved dagger or small sword. Some Sikhs wear a small replica, especially when traveling in airports," Mr. Singh answered. "The right to wear the kirpan, including in federal buildings, has been protected by numerous legal decisions. It is a required article of faith, not a weapon."

"Do women wear these articles too," Jennifer asked.

"The turbans are less common for females, but they do wear a head covering. And yes, they wear the other articles of faith," Mr. Singh answered. "The Sikh faith considers gender equality an important part of the teaching."

What is the Sikh belief of after death?" Stuart asked.

"The Sikh's focus is on this lifetime," Mr. Singh replied. "We are asked to make the best of our time on this earth and to make a connection with God. We do not believe in heaven or hell. Usually at funerals, the body is cremated, and the ashes are returned back to nature in a flowing body of water."

"Okay. Well then, that is all I have. Jennifer?" Stuart turned to her for any further comments.

"I'm good," she replied. "Thank you so much, Mr. Singh. This was very interesting."

"Yes, thank you," Stuart concurred.

"You are welcome anytime," Mr. Singh responded. "*Alavidā*!"

They got in the car and headed out of the driveway. Jennifer's mind was reeling. "How can they not believe in an afterlife if they believe in God?" she blurted out. "I mean, I know I will see my mom again when I die. What about all the stories of near-death experiences? I just don't get it."

"It seems to me that it is a peaceful religion. They help those who are less fortunate," Stuart said calmly. "The founder, Guru Nanuk, was raised a Hindu, I believe, and grew up in a caste system. Hindi believes in reincarnation. Nanuk believed that souls, when ultimately connected to God, were free of the cycle of rebirth."

Jennifer looked over at him. She was about to ask him why he never mentioned that to Mr. Singh. He seemed distracted. His knee was bouncing up and down. *He's nervous,* she thought.

"In about a mile, you are going to turn right by the Starbucks," Stuart instructed.

SIXTEEN

The Homecoming

Jennifer was driving slowly up the street toward the Habib house—Samil's parents. Stuart had been very quiet for the last several blocks. Jennifer glanced over and saw him staring out the window. "Are you ready for this?" she asked.

"I should have done this eight years ago," he replied. "They must hate me."

"Then it's good you are doing this now. And they don't hate you," Jennifer said.

They slowly walked up to the small one-story Cape Cod. The shingled siding looked worn in places. There were rosebushes lining the sidewalk and the front of the house. "I'll bet they smell wonderful in the summer," Jennifer remarked.

"They did; I mean, they do," Stuart answered. He reached the screen door and knocked lightly. Jennifer rolled her eyes at him and reached in front to knock loudly. "You don't need to," Stuart started, but he was interrupted by the door slowly opening. "Hello, Umi," Stuart said to the older woman.

She placed her hand on her heart, and tears filled her eyes. She opened the door and reached out to Stuart, who fell into her hug. She was saying something in Arabic that Jennifer couldn't understand, but she did understand that love was being spoken. Stuart's tears mixed with her own as they held their cheeks together. Stuart pulled away and reached out for Jennifer's hand. "Jennifer," he said, "this is Yara Habib, Sammi's mother. Umi, this is Jennifer Carter, my uh," Stuart paused a split second as he considered what to call Jennifer and then said, "friend." Jennifer started to say hello, but she was taken into an embrace so strongly that she almost couldn't breathe.

"Thank you for bringing him back to me," Yara said over and over again in broken English. "Come in, come in. I will call Ahmed and Amina." The hugging, crying, and laughter happened all over again when Sammi's father and sister arrived. Jennifer found a chair in the corner of the room and sat quietly as the family reconnected.

After a while, Ahmed looked over at her and said, "Jennifer, you must come sit with us. We will speak English now. It is hard to find the right English words for how happy we are that Stuart has come back to us." They ended up staying the night when they realized how very late it was. The next day following breakfast and more tears and hugs, they departed with the promise to come back in a month or two.

"Thanks for driving while I worked on my article," Stuart said shutting his laptop.

"Finished already?" Jennifer asked.

"I'll finish it tonight," Stuart answered. "What are the plans for Billy Graham?"

"How would you like to take the train to North Carolina?" Jennifer asked.

"That sounds interesting," Stuart answered. "I don't think we have the budget for that though."

"It's my treat." Jennifer smiled and continued, "For the first-class ticket home last month. We would get on at Penn Station at about seven in the evening and get into Charlotte at about nine the next morning. We'll drive to Montreat for the interview. We'll leave the next morning."

"Where will we stay?" Stuart asked.

"I have a college roommate there. She said we could stay at her house and use her car. She is going to a conference in Florida," Jennifer said.

"Well, that sounds like a fun adventure," Stuart said, smiling.

"I'm glad you think so because I already got the tickets," Jennifer confessed. "We leave Thursday. Our appointment with Graham is Friday afternoon at two o'clock."

"What would you have done if I had said no?" Stuart asked.

Jennifer laughed. "I would have talked you into it."

"How about I talk you into some lunch before we head into the office?" Stuart said.

"Sounds good," she replied. "I need to drop off the car. Then we can take the subway to Delmonico's. It is another one of my favorite places to eat."

SEVENTEEN

Sikhism: The Light of God Is in All Hearts

Stuart Jones, Editor
(To be published Saturday, October 8, 2011)

> There is but One God, His name is Truth, He is the
> Creator, He fears none, he is without hate, He never
> dies, He is beyond the cycle of births and death, He
> is self-illuminated, He is realized by the kindness of
> the True Guru. He was True in the beginning, He
> was True when the ages commenced and has ever
> been True, He is also True now.
>
> —Guru Nanak

Sikhism is the fifth largest world religion, having just under thirty million followers living in countries all over the world. It began in the Indian province of Punjab about five hundred years ago. Most services today are conducted in Punjabi. Sikh children learn Punjabi as part of their religious education. The founder, Guru Nanak, and his ten successors taught the basic principles of service and *simran*, a Punjabi word meaning remembrance or the continuous act of remembering God. Sikhism is a unique religion and not derived from any other religion. Some scholars suggest that Sikhism is a blend of Islam and Hinduism, but its uniqueness is apparent if you understand the main philosophies and practices.

Sikhs reject many of the practices of Hinduism and Islam. They believe all people are created equal regardless of gender, status, geographic location, or religious affiliation. Sikhs condemn rituals as empty practices. They do not believe in pilgrimages, idolatry, or reverence for pictures. They believe that daily prayer instills understanding and discipline. Their holy scripture teaches that there are many different ways of achieving a connection with God. If you follow the Sikh way, you must follow it to the best of your ability and with absolute devotion. Guru Nanak's message can be summarized as a doctrine of salvation through complete and devoted meditation on God. Salvation is understood in terms of escaping the birth and death rounds of reincarnation so that you can be in a mystical union with God.

Sikhs meet in worship centers called *gurdwaras*. They are centers for worship, education, social activities, celebrations of holidays, and communal meals. The holy scriptures, Guru Granth Sahib, are placed on a high, ornate box-like structure called a palanquin, under a canopy in the middle of one end of the hall. The main activities are held on Sundays and usually one additional day of the week. Before entering the service, worshipers take off their shoes, cover their heads if they have not already done so, and wash their hands in the lobby. There are no clergy per se because the gurus were very clear about each Sikh making his or her own journey. There are *granthis*, teachers who have studied the scriptures extensively, who lead services and perform celebrations. The word *Sikh* means learner or disciple in the Punjabi language. Each Sikh follows his or her own path of devotion and remembrance of God at all times, practices truthful living, equality of humankind, and social justice, and avoids superstitions and blind rituals.

The founder, Guru Nanak, started the practice of keeping hair unshorn. The tenth guru, Godind Singh, implemented The Five Articles of Faith (including uncut hair), which comprises the daily uniform of the Sikh. The turban is part of the uniform because it has spiritual and temporal significance. It is worn out of love and as a mark of commitment to the faith. It covers the unshorn hair. Many Sikh women wear turbans while others cover their hair with scarves. Another article of faith is a comb, called a *kangha*. It can be worn easily in the hair at all times. It is a symbol of cleanliness. The kangha is a spiritual reminder to shed impurities of thought. The third article of faith is a steel bracelet called the *kara*. It is mandatory and meant to be worn at all times. It is a symbol of unbreakable attachment and commitment to God. The fourth article of faith is a religious sword or dagger called *kirpan*. It is a curved single-edged blade that is mandated to be worn at all times. It denotes dignity, self-reliance, and a readiness to defend the weak, oppressed, and Sikh moral values. The fifth article of faith is called *kachera*. They are shorts worn under the outer garment. It reminds the Sikh of the need for self-restraint over passions and desires.

Sikhs believe that remembering God and seeking a connection with the one is the way to spend their time on Earth. They do not believe in heaven or hell or the notion of judgment day. They devote themselves to service and spiritual connection with God in this life.

There are approximately half a million followers of Sikhism in the United States, who are mostly of South Asian origin. They began immigrating in the 1900s as farmers and laborers. During the 1960s, immigration quotas were raised, and trained professionals immigrated in large numbers. There are approximately twenty gurdwaras in the greater metro area. Most gurdwaras have a traditional meal following the service called *langar*. It is cooked and served by the members of the community, and it is open to all visitors of the gurdwara. The meal is shared while sitting on the ground. It has a communal aspect to reinforce the belief that people are equal, irrespective of caste, creed, religion, race, or sex.

EIGHTEEN

The Doctor

"Hi, Mrs. B.," Jennifer said as she was putting her clothes in an overnight bag. "Is Stuart in yet?"

"Not yet, honey. Can I give him a message?" Mrs. B. asked.

"Please tell him I'll meet him at the station this evening. I'm meeting Dad for breakfast, and I have a few things to get done before I leave."

"Okay, honey. Have fun and don't do anything I wouldn't do."

"Mrs. B.!" Jennifer laughed. Jennifer hung up the phone and went into the bathroom to get her toiletries. As she picked up a stack of tampons, she wondered if she would suffer the same fate as her mom. "Primary ovarian insufficiency," the paper had said. She had run across it when going through her mom's files. She wished now that she had talked to her mom about why she had never had any brothers or sisters. She knew now that the reason was because her mother went through menopause when she was in her thirties. All the hormone treatment she went through was the likely cause of her ovarian cancer. Jennifer was going to her family doctor that day to see if it might be the reason her period hadn't come. She was as regular as clockwork, and it was two weeks late. She was feeling fine. She had no hot flashes. She hoped there was a treatment for it if that was the case. She wanted children, and she couldn't bear the thought that she might not be able to have them. *Please, God, let me be okay. Help me not to be anxious,* she prayed silently.

"Hello, Dr. Evans," Jennifer said as the doctor entered the room. Dr. Evans had been her family doctor for two years after the gentle Dr. Goff had retired.

"Hello, Jennifer," Dr. Evans replied. "What brings you in today?"

"I need a referral to a gynecologist," Jennifer said. "I am worried I might have what my mom had—premature menopause."

Dr. Evans looked at her over the rim of her glasses and then down at the paper she was holding. "After looking at the results of your urine test, I rather think I should refer you to an obstetrician, Jennifer. You're pregnant!"

"What?" exclaimed Jennifer. "That's impossible. I've never had intercourse. I," Jennifer paused, remembering the attacker's semen running down the inside of her leg. "I was nearly raped, but the attacker collapsed and ejaculated outside my body."

"It's amazing how resourceful little sperm are when seeking out an egg," Dr. Evans informed her. "When was your last period?"

"Six weeks ago," Jennifer numbly replied, staring ahead into space. "Oh, God, what am I going to do?"

"I can arrange for a termination tomorrow in the pregnancy clinic," Dr. Evans calmly told her.

"An abortion?" Jennifer asked, snapping her head around. "I need to think about this."

"Well, you shouldn't wait too long," Dr. Evans said. "The earlier you have it, the better it is for your recovery."

But not for the baby, she thought. Then she said, "I'm going out of town today. I'll think about it and let you know next week."

"I'll give you numbers for the pregnancy clinic and for Dr. Baker, an obstetrician," Dr. Evans said. "You can make your decision and then give one of them a call. If you decide not to terminate, I advise you to get into an obstetrician right away, considering your family history. I'll send over a referral just in case."

"Thank you," Jennifer said. She slid off the examination table and collected her bag. She walked dazedly out of the building and into the sunlight. In her head, she was going over and over her options about the pregnancy. *If I terminate and have the same early menopause as my mother, I might never have children. If I don't terminate, I will have a terrorist's child. What if the baby turns out like the father?* These were just some of the thoughts she had. Her phone rang. "Hi, Stuart," Jennifer said, coming out of her fog.

"Hey, where are you?" Stuart asked. "I stopped by your apartment on the way to the train station. Are you already there?"

"Oh, gosh!" Jennifer exclaimed, looking at her watch. "I ... I ... I will be there ASAP. I got caught up in my thoughts and didn't realize the time. I have my bag, but I think I left the tickets there," she said as she rifled through her bag.

"Where are you?" Stuart asked. "I'll get the tickets and come to you."

"You know where I hide my key, right?" she asked. "Go in and let me know if you find the tickets. I'll wait on the line."

After a brief pause, Stuart said, "I see them."

"You go on to the station," Jennifer told him. "I'll meet you there. I'm coming from the other direction. See you soon." Jennifer ended the call and looked around for the nearest subway station. *Idiot,* Jennifer thought, chastising herself. Then she started running.

NINETEEN

The Train

The Carolinian was running on time, so Stuart and Jennifer were able to get right on after they met outside the station. The porter showed them to their compartment. "You should go on to the dining car," the porter said, smiling. "It is open another thirty minutes. I'll get your bunks set up."

"Thank you," Stuart and Jennifer said in tandem. They made their way to the dining car and sat down just as the train started moving. Their natural response to the movement had them looking out the window.

"Hello, folks," the waiter said as he approached their table. "Did you just get on?" he asked.

"Yes," Stuart replied, smiling. His smile faded as he looked at Jennifer and saw her continuing to stare out the window. She looked like she was somewhere else.

"You can put your order together on this form," the waiter said, pulling out a form from his book. "Would you like wine or beer?"

"I'd like red wine," Stuart replied. "Jennifer? Jennifer," he said again when she didn't answer him.

"Hmmm?" she responded, turning to look up at the waiter.

"Would you like wine?" Stuart asked.

"No, thanks. I'll just have water," she responded.

They ordered. After the waiter brought them their food, Stuart took Jennifer's hand and said, "Is something the matter? You seem very distracted."

"I can't talk about it right now, Stuart," Jennifer said. "Let me think about it some more. I'll tell you later." *Or not,* she thought. They finished eating in silence and walked back to their compartment. There wasn't enough room to move inside the tiny bathroom, so when Stuart went in to relieve himself, she quickly put on her pajama pants and T-shirt and climbed into the bottom bunk. They had spent the last couple of hours in near silence, pretending to read or look at their phones. All the while, they felt the other's apprehension and disquiet.

"Good night," Stuart said as he climbed into the top bunk.

"Good night, Stuart," Jennifer said quietly. She thought, *Why don't I just tell him? He, of all people, would understand. He hasn't pressed me to talk. He knows something is wrong. Maybe he can help me make a decision.* "Stuart," she said. And just like that, he climbed down to the bottom bunk, sat facing her, and held her hands in his. *Should I just blurt out the words, "I'm pregnant," or start with why I went to the doctor in the first place,* she thought. She decided on the latter.

"My mother was unable to have any more children after me because she went through early menopause. She was in her thirties. It is a rare condition for someone that young," she began. "I went to the doctor today because my period was late. I was afraid I was going through early menopause like my mother."

"But you're only twenty-two," Stuart said gently.

"You're right, and I'm not going through menopause," Jennifer continued. "Actually, I'm ... pregnant," she said, finally getting the words out and feeling relieved. "I don't know what to do," she said teary-eyed and put her head in her hands, waiting for Stuart's reaction. Stuart pulled her into his lap and held her in a tight hug. She cried in earnest now and held onto him. "I've never had intercourse, Stuart, but—"

"And lo, a virgin shall conceive," Stuart interrupted.

"Stop it, Stuart. It's nothing like that. I'm going to have a terrorist's baby," she said as more tears welled up in her eyes. "You believe me, though, that I am or was a virgin?"

"I kind of knew when the doctor said the hymen was mostly intact," Stuart said. "And I'm glad you're not thinking about an abortion, right?"

"I was given that option. But what if I do go through early menopause? What if this is my only chance of a child?" Jennifer answered.

They sat holding each other for a long while as the rocking motion of the train calmed their thoughts. He pulled back and looked into her eyes, "Jennifer, this isn't a terrorist's baby; it will be our baby." She looked at him with a puzzled expression on her face. "Marry me, Jennifer," he said with a hopeful look on his face. "I love you."

"I don't know what to say," she said and sniffed.

"Say yes," Stuart told her. "Please say yes."

"I like you Stuart, a lot. I feel safe with you. You are hardworking. You don't snore. You are certainly good-looking," she said, listing a few more of his attributes while his smile grew. "I think I can marry you." Then he kissed her. They wrapped their arms around each other while the kiss deepened. They lay down on the small bunk and entwined their legs. She was starting to feel an urge so powerful that she pulled away gasping and said, "I think you're going to be a wonderful lover too."

They sat up laughing. "Let's get married tomorrow," Stuart blurted out. North Carolina doesn't have a waiting period after you get a license."

"How would you know that?" Jennifer asked.

"Jo Jo. You remember him, right?" he asked. "He got married on leave when we were in Afghanistan. He only had a three-day pass, so they went to North Carolina. Debbie was from South Carolina. Do you think Billy Graham will marry us?"

"Oh, no, Stuart," Jennifer said. "We can't ask him.

TWENTY

The Evangelist

"I can't tell you what an honor it is that you would meet with us," Stuart said, shaking the hand of the famous Billy Graham. He was rather surprised that he had answered the door. "This is my friend Jennifer Carter," Stuart said.

"Come in before you freeze to death," Mr. Graham said. "Would you like some coffee?"

"Yes, thank you," they responded in tandem. They hung up their coats and followed the elderly Graham down the hall to the kitchen. When the coffee was served and they were sitting around the kitchen table, Stuart pulled out his recorder and notepad to start the interview.

"Tell me a little bit about yourself, Stuart," Mr. Graham said before Stuart could ask his first question.

"Ah, well," Stuart spoke hesitantly. "I'm just starting my career in the newspaper business." *I hope he doesn't ask me if I'm saved,* he thought.

"I've read a couple of your articles," Graham said and turned to Jennifer. "I know your father, Jennifer, did he tell you that?"

"I know that he saw you in Germany at one of your crusades, but he didn't tell me that you knew each other," Jennifer said, surprised.

"Ruth and I had dinner with your dad and mom sometime in the sixties, but I've forgotten the date," Graham said. "I was sad to hear of your mom's passing."

"That's kind of you," Jennifer replied. "I remember my mom watching your sermons on TV. You've led millions of people to Christ."

"I have tried to remain faithful to what God wanted me to do—preach the gospel," Graham replied, smiling.

"I'm going to do a multipart column on Christianity," Stuart told the reverend, "sort of in reverse order—Protestantism then Catholicism. I know historically it happened the other way around. Your career has been spent taking your message to the world, much like the original apostles, so your insights on Christianity would be very helpful."

"It's not my message," Graham interjected. "It's God's message. It doesn't matter if you're Catholic or Protestant. All churches have a cross, either on their buildings or in their buildings. That's the one thing all Christians believe. Jesus died on the cross as an atonement for sin. He did it for you, for me, for anyone. The resurrection of Christ inspired the disciples to go and tell the whole world that Jesus was alive. That was the beginning of Christianity."

"Why are there so many different denominations, if that is the main point of the religion?" Stuart asked.

"One reason there are so many different denominations in our nation is because we live in a country that practices religious freedom," Graham replied. "This wasn't true several hundred years ago in many countries. Then only one church was tolerated in most nations. When people immigrated here, they were free to bring their own religious practices with them, and they did. Other churches came into existence because of some minor disagreement over doctrine or to meet the needs of a particular group of people. Sadly, sometimes churches have been started because of conflict between members. In spite of this, all Christian churches agree on the central truths of the gospel: We are sinners in need of God's forgiveness. Jesus Christ came down from heaven to save us from our sins. By his death on the cross, the power of the cross, and his resurrection, we can have eternal life. He alone is our hope and our source of everlasting joy and peace. Have you committed your life to Him?"

"I, er ... I," Stuart mumbled.

"Stuart was raised a Muslim," Jennifer interjected.

"In the Qur'an," Stuart began, "Jesus is described as the Messiah, born of a virgin, performing miracles, accompanied by disciples, rejected by the Jewish establishment but not as crucified or resurrected. Rather, he was miraculously saved by God and ascended into heaven. Jesus is one of the most important prophets, and he will return in the Second Coming, but he is not considered divine or the son of God. There is only one God."

"If he is not divine, then how can he return?" Graham asked.

"His return will be a sign of the end times," Stuart said. "He will clear all the confusion prevailing in the world regarding his life and mission. He will follow the law of God as perfected by the final prophet."

"We agree on a couple of things," Graham told Stuart. "Jesus was the long-awaited Messiah, he will come again, and there will be no more confusion. I believe that he *is* the Son of the living God and that he is alive today. He is one of the persons in the Trinity: God the Father, God the Son, and God the Holy Spirit. God in three different realities. Christians do not worship multiple gods."

"I always think about water when I think about the Trinity," Jennifer said. Both men turned to look at her. "Water has three forms: ice, liquid, and steam. All matter really exists as liquid, solid, and gas, depending on external forces. If God is the external force, he can be whatever he wants."

"Jesus Christ was God in human form," Graham said. "The Holy Spirit lives inside us when we accept Jesus and helps us grow closer to God. The opening verses in the gospel of John tell us, 'In the beginning was the Word, and the Word was with God, and the Word was God. He was with God in the beginning. Through him all things were made; without him nothing was made that has been made.' Then later in John chapter 15 verse 26, he writes, 'When the Helper has come, whom I will send to you from the Father, the Spirit of truth, who proceeds from the Father, he will testify about me.'"

"Do you have the Bible memorized or at least the New Testament?" Stuart asked.

"No, even though I spent my entire life reading and studying the Bible," Graham answered. "I wish I knew more of it. But the Bible is not just for preachers and scholars. The Bible is God's Word to everyone. It provides nourishment to hearts and souls. God's promises can give you strength for today and for the future."

"What age were you when you chose Christianity?" Stuart asked.

"I like the way you asked that," Graham replied. "We can choose or not choose to believe in the resurrection and ask Jesus to forgive our sins. I chose to follow Christ in 1934. God had a plan for my life. He has a plan for your life too."

"I don't know if I like the plan God has for my life right now," Jennifer blurted out and immediately regretted it. "I mean ... I ..." She looked at Stuart, who smiled and nodded. Just like that, she told Billy Graham what had happened to her. For the next thirty minutes, she and Stuart laid out what had happened in Saudi Arabia, subsequently ending with their plan to marry. They consented when Mr. Graham asked them if he could pray with them.

"Jennifer, isn't it better facing this struggle with God than without him?" Graham asked.

"Definitely," she replied. "I should be devastated, but somehow, I'm not. I believe everything will turn out all right."

"Stuart," Graham said. "I believe God's plan put you in Jennifer's life, but it shouldn't be what I believe. It should be what you believe."

"Thank you," Stuart said. "You've given me a lot to think about."

Mr. Graham picked up his cell phone and started scrolling. "Now let me call Todd to come over now. He is the Presbyterian minister at the church just down the road. He and his wife usually stop by at suppertime to see how I'm getting on. I'm not licensed to sign marriage certificates anymore. Todd can marry you, and his wife and I will be your witnesses. How would that work for you?"

Stuart and Jennifer held hands all the way back to Charlotte. They had opted for traditional wedding vows. Jennifer blushed after their kiss, which lasted a little longer than necessary. Reverend Miller had to clear his throat a couple of times before they stopped. Just thinking about it made her blush again. They parked the car in the garage, but he stopped her from shutting the garage door.

"Let's go through the front door," Stuart said, pulling her along behind him. When they reached the front door, he unlocked it and then swept her up in his arms to carry her over the threshold. Jennifer laughed all the way up the stairs.

It's a good thing my friend is out of town this weekend, she thought. Sometime during the night when they came up for air, Stuart had the good sense to shut the garage door. Later, they had to speed to the train station and run to catch the train because of their last-minute lovemaking session.

"I wish we had a sleeper car on the way back," Stuart said as he helped her off the platform and up the train steps.

"Why don't we ask the porter if there is one available," Jennifer said. There was.

"Good karma," Stuart said as they shut the cabin door and raced to remove their clothes. Jennifer giggled at his comment, but her laughter soon turned to moans.

TWENTY-ONE

Christianity, Part I: The Great Commission

Stuart Jones, Editor
(To be published Saturday, November 12, 2011)

> Jesus came to them and spoke to them, saying, "All authority has been given to me in heaven and on earth. Go and make disciples of all nations, baptizing them in the name of the Father and of the Son and of the Holy Spirit, teaching them to observe all things that I commanded you. Behold, I am with you always, even to the end of the age."
> —Matthew 28:18–20

Christianity is the largest religion in the world, having more than two billion followers. It originated with the eyewitness accounts of the death and resurrection of Jesus Christ in the first century. The largest groups are the Roman Catholic, Eastern Orthodox, and Protestant churches. The latter group is the most diverse, having thousands of separate churches, sects, and denominations. Even given the diversity in the denominations, all Christians believe in the trifold nature of God: God the Father, God the Son, and God the Holy Spirit.

All groups use the Holy Bible as a source of historical events leading up to Jesus's birth as the Messiah (Old Testament), his miraculous works and instructions given to his followers, and the firsthand accounts of his life and teachings as referenced by his disciples (New Testament). The thirty-nine books of the Old Testament already existed at the time of Jesus, which is what he referred to as the scriptures. At the time the early church was forming, Jesus's disciples and followers started putting together historical records of his life, as was witnessed or passed down in telling. His followers Paul and Peter wrote letters to the churches they established, which were distributed throughout congregations in Europe and Asia.

Church leaders gathered between AD 325 and 381 to evaluate the validity of the writings and to determine which books or letters would be included in the New Testament. Twenty-seven books were chosen to make up the New Testament based on whether the writing was written by one of Jesus's disciples, someone who was a witness to his ministry, or someone who interviewed witnesses (such as Luke). The writings chosen were all written in the first century and were known to be consistent with other portions of the valid Bible. The first compilation of Old and New Testament scripture was put together by Jerome, an early Christian priest and theologian. It was written in Latin. Some denominations recognize other writings that are not included in the Bible to be within the canon of Holy Scripture. Christians believe that the Bible is God's word to everyone and that it provides nourishment to the soul.

The Reformation began in the early sixteenth century when Martin Luther published his ninety-five theses, arguing for the biblical truth of salvation by grace through faith in Jesus Christ alone. Following this, the Protestant faith separated from the Roman Catholic church, which paved the way to a more faithful understanding of scripture by anyone who wished to study. Martin Luther wasn't the only reformer. Zwingli and Calvin in Switzerland, Henry VIII in England, and John Knox in Scotland were all instrumental in reforming the way Christianity was practiced by the masses.

What exactly was reformed by these leaders of the practice of Christianity? First and foremost, the scriptures were meant to be read and heard by all people in their own languages. Luther went on to translate the Bible into German, John Calvin translated the Bible into French, and William Tyndale did this in English. Next, worship itself was reformed. Believers weren't required to pay indulgences to the church for salvation. Songs, prayers, and sermons were all based on scriptures. Lastly, idol worship and distinctions between laity and the priesthood were removed.

The church can never be better than its teachers and shepherds. James the brother of Jesus seemed to understand the need for a very high standard in the ministry. He said, "Let not many of you be teachers, my brothers, knowing that we will receive heavier judgment" (James 3:1). During the upheaval of the reformation, the goal was not to tear down but to build up and to bring the people of God back to the heart and center of worship. Luther wanted to put the focus back on the person and work of Christ as revealed in the preaching of God's Word. All worship is essentially a response to the character of God as revealed in his work of redemption. In the Old Testament, it means remembering Passover and the Exodus. In the New Testament, it means remembering the cross and the empty tomb. In these events, the Lord is revealed in all his glory and goodness.

Christianity may appear simple to understand when one focuses on the life of Jesus as the central figure. In reality, it is more complicated in that the vast majority of Christians focus their faith on the God of the here and now. Integral to the belief of Christians is acceptance of the fact that

1. Humans are sinners.
2. Jesus (God in human form) willingly died on the cross for all humankind to atone for our sins.
3. This grace and forgiveness are freely given.
4. Salvation and the prospect of eternal life are attained by accepting this grace by asking Jesus to enter your life.

Some denominations do not require action on the part of the sinner. Grace is bestowed. The choice to follow Christ will be reflected in the life of the believer. The believer accepts the miracle of the resurrection by faith.

> For by grace, you have been saved through faith, and that not of yourselves; it is the gift of God. (Ephesians 2:8)

> Being therefore justified by faith, we have peace with God through our Lord Jesus Christ. (Romans 5:1)

In a recent interview with the Reverend Billy Graham, he told me, "Jesus is the long-awaited Messiah, he will come again, and there will be no more confusion. I believe he *is* the Son of the living God and is alive today. He is one of the persons in the Trinity: God the Father, God the Son, and God the Holy Spirit. He is God in three different realities. Christians do not worship multiple gods. Jesus Christ was God in human form. The Holy Spirit lives inside us when we accept Jesus and helps us grow closer to God. We can choose or not choose to believe in the resurrection and ask Jesus to forgive our sins. God has a plan for your life, and the sooner you accept his grace, the sooner you will receive the peace that passes all understanding."

There are thousands of Christian churches in the greater metro area to choose from. Just because you have tried one church and haven't liked it doesn't mean there isn't a church where you will feel at home. We will continue the discussion of Christianity next month when we explore the Roman Catholic faith.

TWENTY-TWO

The Ultrasound

"I'm going with you to tell your father," Stuart told Jennifer the morning after their train trip home. He had stayed in her apartment. He was glad that Henry hadn't paid Jen a surprise visit. Their night of lovemaking had been spectacular. They were having coffee and bagels in the living room on the floor because the couch cushions were askew. The dining table was full of her mom's boxes, which Jennifer had brought home.

"I don't think that is a good idea," Jennifer said. "Remember how uncivil he was toward you at the office? This will certainly be an escalation."

"He'll get over it," Stuart replied after kissing the corner of her mouth to remove some cream cheese.

"Come to church with me then, and we can tell him at lunch," Jennifer said purposefully, leaving more cream cheese on her lips.

When they got to church, Henry barked in a whisper, "You're late!" as Jennifer leaned down to kiss him on the cheek. Only then did he see Stuart. He frowned. They squeezed into the pew just as everyone was standing for the first song.

"Stuart is doing research on Christianity," Jennifer told her dad as they were exiting the church. "Where shall we eat?"

"Stuart," Henry acknowledged Stuart tersely.

"Henry," Stuart replied brightly.

"How was the visit with Billy Graham?" Henry asked.

"Dad!" Jennifer exclaimed. "You didn't tell me that you and Mom knew him."

"Well, I've hardly seen you these last few weeks," Henry responded. "It slipped my mind when we were together, and it wasn't a good time to tell you when I remembered."

"He told me that you and Mom had dinner with him and his wife in Germany," Jennifer said.

"Yes, those were fun times," Henry recalled. They arrived at the diner and gave their names to the hostess. "You want to tell me what this is really about?" Henry said as they waited in the corner for their table.

"Wow, he really does read you like a book," Stuart told Jennifer. Stuart waited for Jennifer to say something. She looked like she couldn't find the right words.

"Jenny?" Henry said.

"We got married on Friday, Henry," Stuart blurted out, "in North Carolina—at Billy Graham's house."

"Jenny?" Henry said, still looking at Jennifer.

Jennifer moved closer to Stuart, who put his arm around her shoulder. "I'm pregnant with the kidnapper's baby," Jennifer whispered so that only her dad and Stuart heard.

"Carter!" the hostess announced.

"Your dad took it a lot better than I thought he would," Stuart told Jennifer as they waited in the doctor's office two weeks later.

"I feel like I hurt his feelings," Jennifer replied.

"Jennifer, he loves you," Stuart said. "He wants you to be happy. He'll get over the fact that it's me you are in love with. I mean, you are in love with me, right?"

"Deliriously so," Jennifer said, looking into his eyes. She nearly kissed him except she heard her name called by the nurse. They followed her back to the patient room.

"When was your last period?" the nurse asked as she plotted Jennifer's vital signs in her chart.

"Mid-August, but I know the day I got pregnant—August 26," Jennifer answered.

The nurse looked over her glasses at Jennifer. "You're that sure?"

"I won't go into detail, but yes, I'm that sure," Jennifer answered.

There was a knock at the door, and the doctor entered the room. "Hello Mr. and Mrs. Jones. I'm Dr. Baker," he announced as she shook both of their hands. I got your referral from Dr. Evans. Why don't you lie back, and we'll take a peek at who you've got in there." The nurse stood on one side and put some cold jelly on her abdomen. She also put an instrument on her belly. Immediately, there were whoosh-whoosh sounds. The doctor stood on the other side and placed a wand on her belly. The monitor was just out of view from Jennifer and Stuart, who stood by her head. The doctor ran the wand up and down her belly and looked puzzled. After about twenty minutes, she finally turned the monitor around so that Jennifer and Stuart could see it. "It would appear that you have multiple fetuses," the doctor told them. "I can't be certain, but I think I count at least four. It seems that they are of different gestational ages. When did you become pregnant again?"

"August 26, about twelve weeks ago," Jennifer whispered. She was squeezing Stuart's hand tightly.

"It sounds like there are multiple heartbeats," the nurse said, concentrating on the screen.

The doctor put down the wand and wiped Jennifer's belly with a cloth. She helped Jennifer sit up. "I'll need to see you back in a couple of weeks," she said. "This is likely going to be a multiple-birth scenario, which will necessitate transfer to a high-risk OB. I need to do a little reading to be sure, but I think you might have a condition called superfecundation. I personally have never seen it, not even in residency. I have only read a few accounts."

"What does that mean?" Stuart asked.

"It means that you can get pregnant while already pregnant, to put it in simple terms," Dr. Baker replied. "It is an extremely rare condition where the body releases an egg after an embryo is already implanted in the uterus. Under normal conditions your body should have ramped up production of estrogen, progesterone, and HCG to support pregnancy, which should have inhibited further egg production."

"Can you tell which embryo is the oldest?" Jennifer asked, looking at Stuart instead of Dr. Baker.

"Not at this stage," Dr. Baker answered.

Stuart gave Jennifer a hug. They both smiled at each other. "Wow," Jennifer said.

TWENTY-THREE

The Priest

"Hello, everyone," Stuart said, bringing the meeting to order. "I have some big news to share."

"Congratulations," Abe said as he got up and gave Jennifer a hug.

Stuart stared at Abe slack-jawed and asked, "How did you know?"

"Know what?" everyone asked almost in unison.

"Jennifer and Stuart got married," Abe said. Everyone stood and congratulated Stuart and Jennifer with hugs and kisses.

"No, really," Stuart said to Abe. "How did you know?"

"I have a cousin who is the secretary for Montreat Presbyterian Church," Abe replied. "Small world, huh?"

Stuart just shook his head and said, "I suppose you have read my next article too?"

"Yeah, very insightful," Abe replied.

"Would you write a piece on the Reformation?" Stuart asked, sighing at the apparent clairvoyance of his writer.

"Sure thing," Abe replied. "I might even pull the last one Enid did several years ago if that's okay. She did a great job with it."

"Sure," Stuart said. "No need to reinvent the wheel."

"Jennifer, honey," Mrs. B. piped up, "do you want to share the rest of your news?"

Stuart looked at her with raised eyebrows. "I might as well," Jennifer said. "They are going to know soon enough."

"Greetings, all." Henry Carter burst into the room. He started handing out cigars. "I'm going to be a grandfather," he said gleefully.

"I guess he did take it well," Stuart whispered to Jennifer as the group burst into applause.

"He said he talked to my mother about it, and she told him he better be the best grandfather ever," Jennifer whispered back.

"Talked to your mom?" Stuart questioned.

"Don't ask," Jennifer said, turning to the others in the room, who wanted to give her more hugs.

"Okay, okay," Stuart said elevating his voice so that the room would calm down. "Abe, since you are using Enid's article on reformation, could you put together something on Hanukkah for next month?"

"Done," Abe said.

"Enid," Stuart continued, "I think there is a Sikh celebration coming up soon. Could you check it out and write a brief article on it?"

"Sure, Stuart," Enid replied. "I think there is also a Buddhist celebration coming up. I'll write about it too."

"Thanks," Stuart said, smiling. "Mrs. B., how are our numbers?"

"Accounting thinks we are responsible for at least 8 percent of increased sales," Mrs. B. reported. "When we get to 10 percent, I think we might get our own page."

"Great news," Stuart said. "Thanks. Jennifer, did you book the priest?"

"Yes. He finally got back with me," Jennifer responded. "We'll meet him at the diocese office on Thursday."

"Thank you for meeting with us," Stuart said, shaking the cardinal's hand. "Do I call you Cardinal Eagan?"

"That would suffice," Cardinal Eagan replied.

"Thank you," Stuart said. "I have a pretty good idea of how Christianity got started and of the two schisms in early Catholicism—the Eastern Orthodox church and Protestantism. What I want you to discuss are the origins of the Roman Catholic church and its presence today. I believe the Roman Catholic faith is the largest Christian denomination in the world. It is certainly the largest faith group in the greater metro area."

"Quite right," Eagan said. "One in four people in the world is Catholic. And you can drop the word Roman; it is Catholic church."

"Isn't it centered in Rome?" Stuart asked.

"Well, the pope resides there in Vatican City," Eagan replied. "But it is centered in whatever location Christ's church resides. In Matthew 16:18, Christ told the apostle Simon, after he declared Jesus to be the Messiah, 'I also tell you that you are Peter, and on this rock I will build my church, and the gates of Hades will not prevail against it.' After Christ's death and resurrection and during the beginnings of the early church, everyone looked to Peter for answers and decisions about how to proceed. He was the first bishop in Rome and was followed by Pope Linus and a series of successors up to Pope Benedict today. Peter spent the last years of his life in Rome. He was martyred there. St. Paul, who evangelized to the Gentiles, spent the last years of his life in Rome also. The graves of Saint Peter and Saint Paul are in Rome. The Roman emperor Constantine the Great became a Christian, legalizing Christianity. He convened the Council of Nicaea, which produced a belief statement called the Nicene Creed in AD 325. It is still used today. The significant happenings in Rome during the early days of Christianity made it the natural administrative center that it is today.

Cardinal Eagan continued, "The Catholic church is the only

one that can claim to have been founded by Christ personally. Every other church traces its lineage back to a human person, such as Martin Luther or John Wesley. The Catholic church can trace its lineage back to Jesus Christ. Throughout history and even with the separation of the Eastern Orthodox and Protestant churches, the Catholic church has remained the evangelical driving force, as the original apostles intended. The Holy Spirit first came to the early believers at Pentecost. You can read about it in the book of Acts."

"Can you tell me about the Eucharist and transubstantiation?" Jennifer asked.

"Are you familiar with the term mystical body of Christ, which is how some refer to the Catholic church?" Eagan asked.

"I've not heard of it," Jennifer answered. Stuart shook his head no.

"The term mystical body of Christ is used because its members are united by supernatural bonds with one another and Christ. Christ is the head, and believers are the body, through the power of the Holy Spirit. What the soul is to the body, the Holy Spirit is to the church. Instead of organization, the church is more like an organism. It has an internal means of subsistence, which is the Holy Eucharist.

"You do think that the bread and wine are the actual body and blood of Christ, though, right?" Jennifer asked.

Cardinal Eagan smiled. "Think of your life or the life of your baby," he said, gesturing to her swollen abdomen. "Our exterior is constantly changing. We all look much different now than when we were first conceived. What remains unchanged is who we are at our core—a distinct human being with a soul. In other words, our exteriors change, but our substance remains the same. With the Eucharist, it's just the opposite. While the exterior of the bread and wine—taste, texture, and appearance—do not change, the substance does change. It still looks, feels, and tastes like bread and wine, but it has truly become the body and blood of Christ. Jesus is present in a real and substantial manner. This is what the Catholic church means by transubstantiation."

Cardinal Eagan continued, "When we receive the Eucharist, we are receiving Jesus, who is fully God and fully man. This mystery is something that is revealed by God, but it is not readily understandable by human reason alone. By receiving the Eucharist, we are making a promise to love and obey God. We are receiving the grace necessary to do God's will. We grow in faith each time we receive."

"When was the Eucharist first introduced to the church service?" Stuart asked.

"It was about two thousand years ago at the Last Supper," the cardinal replied. "Jesus and the apostles were gathered together in what was Jesus's final meal before his crucifixion. It is reported all four Gospel writings, but Matthew, Mark, and Luke detail the specific sharing of bread and wine, with the instructions to do this in his memory."

"What instructions?" Stuart asked.

Cardinal Eagan replied, "For example, Luke writes in chapter 22 verses 19–21, 'He took bread, and when he had given thanks, he broke, and gave it to them, saying, "This is my body which is given for you. Do this in memory of me." Likewise, he took the cup after supper, saying "This cup is the new covenant in my blood, which is poured out for you."'" A covenant, in this context, is a type of relationship.

The whole purpose of Mass is to worship God, to unite ourselves with the sacrifice of Jesus, and to elevate our lives to the life of God. All the liturgy, songs, smells, readings are centered on the receiving of Christ's body and blood. We will only get out of this relationship with God what we put into it. God's grace can only work in our lives if we are open to receiving it. A short homily is spoken to encourage the members to go and live like Christ would have us live."

"Are there other ways that worshippers can interact with God? Does it always involve a priest?" Stuart asked.

"There are seven sacraments, which are ways that priests intercede or bring grace from God to ordinary people," the cardinal explained. "Besides the Eucharist, there is baptism, confirmation, confession, anointing of the sick, marriage, and holy orders. The latter is only received by those joining the priesthood. Anyone can pray without the help of a priest, and an active prayer life is encouraged. Daily prayer and reading the Bible go hand in hand."

"Why aren't priests allowed to marry?" Stuart asked.

"In the early church, some of the apostles and priests were married," Cardinal Eagan explained. "But very early on, around AD 300, the church was aware that celibacy was extremely important. Ask any married clergy whether it is difficult to have two families—his natural family and his congregation. By remaining celibate and devoting themselves to the service of the church, priests more closely model Christ."

Jennifer asked, "What is the Catholic view of life after death?"

"Death is the separation of body and soul," the cardinal responded. "Each of us will be judged by Christ based on our life's conduct. Before we enter heaven and full communion with God, every trace of sin within us must be expunged. This state is called purgatory. It is not a place but rather a condition of existence. To share the divine life, we must be pure. Christ is our intercessor, who atones for us. As sinners, we will confess and ask him to purify or cleanse us of the stain of sin. He will also judge those who refuse the Father's love and forgiveness."

"But we will see our loved ones again," Jennifer asked, but actually it came out as a statement.

"Those who enjoy the state of purification with the heavenly Father will unite with those who already enjoy the fullness of eternal life. Just as earthly believers unite in the mystical body, those who unite in heaven do so as well."

"Thank you," Stuart said, rising to shake the cardinal's hand.

"Good luck to you. Go with the peace of God," Cardinal Eagan said, making the sign of the cross in the air.

"Goodbye," Jennifer said as she left the office with Stuart's hand on her shoulder.

TWENTY-FOUR

The Specialist

"Good afternoon," Dr. Anderson said as she came into the room. "I'm Dr. Anderson. Dr. Baker referred you to me due to your multiple fetuses. I admit, I deal with multiple births exclusively, but this case is certainly challenging due to the various gestational ages of the fetuses. I recommend we do another ultrasound because it has been two months since your last one. How does that sound?"

"Sounds good," Stuart and Jennifer said in unison. They looked at each other and smiled.

"Rebecca, could you please come in to assist?" Dr. Anderson said into the phone intercom. A nurse walked into the room. Jennifer lay back. She was covered with a sheet, and then the nurse squeezed lubricating jelly onto her swollen belly.

"Ooh, that's cold." Jennifer shivered.

"How are you feeling?" Dr. Anderson asked Jennifer.

"Great," Jennifer answered. "I'm not sick anymore in the morning. I'm sure to eat something with the vitamin. I still get tired at the end of the day."

"You're at five months post-initial pregnancy," Dr. Anderson stated. "You show more than a typical five-month pregnancy, but that is to be expected."

"I'm definitely wearing maternity clothes," Jennifer said.

The doctor looked at the screen a for long time. It was so long that Stuart went around to look over her shoulder. "I'm recording and taking pictures as I go," Dr. Anderson told him. I believe you have seven fetuses."

"Seven!" Jennifer exclaimed.

"Lucky number seven," Stuart quipped.

"I wouldn't be that optimistic about the luck of the youngest fetuses," Dr. Anderson said. "Have you been wearing a condom during intercourse?" she asked Stuart.

"Yes, for the last couple of months," he said, turning serious. "And what do you mean by not being optimistic?" He reached for Jennifer's hand.

"Hopefully, we can get you to full term or beyond," Dr. Anderson told Jennifer. "It might be that the larger babies squeeze out the younger ones, who may not develop properly or get adequate nutrients. At best, they will be anywhere from four-to-seven months gestational age by the time you go into labor. It is my recommendation that we plan on C-section before or when you start labor. I also want you to consider the possibility of removing the youngest two fetuses in order to allow the oldest to have a better chance of survival."

"I can't do that," Jennifer said. "I just can't do that. Stuart, please tell her we can't do that."

Holding her hand up, Dr. Anderson said calmly, "If it isn't something you'd consider, we will take it off the table right now. The important thing is for you to do everything possible to make it the full nine months so that the youngest fetuses will have the best chance of survival. At any signs of cramping or discomfort, you need to contact me. I will probably put you on bed rest for the last couple of months as it is. I'm going to take some blood samples, too, for routine screenings. You gave a urine sample at check-in, didn't you?"

"Yes," Jennifer said.

"It was normal," the nurse said. "I hadn't got it charted yet.

"Okay," Dr. Anderson said as she wiped off the jelly from Jennifer's stomach. "Give me a minute to print out the photos for you, and you can be on your way. Make an appointment for three weeks, but you know to come in sooner should you have any concerns or cramping."

"Thank you, doctor," Jennifer said sitting up. The doctor and nurse left the room, and Jennifer turned to Stuart.

"You've been awfully quiet," she said, holding on to him to get off the table.

"I guess I am in shock," he said. "Seven at once. How are we ever going to manage?"

"Would you care if I invited dad to dinner tonight so he can help us brainstorm?" Jennifer asked.

"I think that would be a great idea," Stuart answered. "I wish your mom were still here. Wouldn't she love this?"

"Yes," Jennifer said, tearing up. "She would know just what to do."

They held each other for a long time. The nurse knocked and entered with an envelope.

"Here you go," she said. "I have a disc in here, too, with a short video clip. It is hard to tell the exact location of each fetus. They will get more recognizable with each ultrasound."

"Thank you," Stuart said, taking the envelope. "Come on. Let's call your dad."

TWENTY-FIVE

The Swami

"Jennifer, honey, why are you here?" Mrs. B. said when she came round the corner and saw Jennifer with Stuart.

"I can either sit around the house or sit around here. I'm not lonely here," Jennifer told her and gave her a hug.

Stuart led her to her desk, where she sat in her new X-chair with rollers. He then proceeded to push her into the conference room.

"Here you go, Jen," Abe said, handing her a cup of coffee.

"Thanks, Abe," Jennifer said, smiling. "You make the best coffee, so I was holding out until I got to work."

"How are you feeling?" Enid asked concernedly.

"Other than feeling like an elephant, I feel great," Jennifer replied. "Stuart won't let me do anything other than sit around the house."

"As he should," Enid and Mrs. B. said in unison. Everyone laughed.

"Okay, let's get started," Stuart said, sitting down next to Jennifer. "Mrs. B., how are the numbers looking?"

"It was a good idea of Jennifer's to just advertise Christmas and holiday programs for the December spread," Mrs. B. said. "We doubled our monthly revenue and sales have been steadily inching up."

"Excellent," Stuart said. Turning to Jennifer he asked, "Any luck with a Hindu faith leader?"

"We have an appointment with a priest from the Central Hindu Cultural Center next Tuesday," Jennifer said. She held up her hand just as Stuart started to speak. "I asked him to come here for the interview because I knew you wouldn't let me go with you if we went to the temple," she said.

"I thought they were called Swami," Stuart said.

"Swami refers to a monastic spiritual leader who has taken a vow of celibacy," Jennifer explained. "They study and write and are seldom involved in the day-to-day religious practices of the temple."

"How do you know this?" Stuart asked.

"Priest Bhattar told me when I called," Jennifer answered.

"Hello, everyone," Henry said as he swept into the room. He bent down to give Jennifer a kiss on the cheek. "How are my grandchildren?" he asked her.

"Fine, Dad. They're fine. I'm fine," Jennifer said.

"Stuart," Henry said turning to Stuart, "I got a call from Cardinal Eagan complimenting you on your interview and article. Did you send him the article? It doesn't run until Friday."

"If I wasn't Jewish, it would turn me Catholic," Abe said.

Stuart turned to look at Abe. "How do you do it?" Abe just shrugged and winked at Jennifer as he took a sip of his coffee. "I wanted to be sure I got the mystical body of Christ wording correct," Stuart told Henry. "I didn't want to be a source of confusion if it wasn't correct."

"Well, okay then. I'll leave you to it," Henry said, turning toward the door. Turning back, he asked, "Did you get hold of your mother?"

"I've left her a couple of messages," Stuart responded. "I'm sure she'll get back with me soon." Stuart stood and passed out a list of article suggestions. "These are just suggestions. Please look them over, pick two or three or add your own, and let me know what you want to write about. I'm sure there are some celebrations I am missing. Thank you, everyone. We'll meet again in a month—I hope," Stuart added. He wheeled Jennifer back out to her desk so that she could put her feet up and use her keyboard from her chair.

"Thank you for coming to meet us here," Stuart told Sri Bhattar, who placed his palms together and bowed instead of shaking Stuart's outstretched hand. Stuart returned the gesture.

"It intrigues me that you want to learn about our religion," the priest replied. "The world has come to call it Hinduism, but the correct way to refer to our religion is *Sanatan dharma*. It has existed since the beginning of time. It has no prophet or founder."

"What was that you called it?" Stuart interrupted.

"Sanatan dharma," the priest replied. It is Sanskrit, and it means everlasting duty or forever duty.

"Duty," Stuart said. "What specific duties are required?"

The priest smiled and said, "Duty to God forever. Followers may follow different paths to God, but the core beliefs are the same."

"What are the core beliefs?" Jennifer asked.

"Belief in one supreme God and in the holy scriptures, which are called Vedas. All paths lead to a common goal of salvation, which is the soul's freedom from a temporary body or moksha or nirvana as Buddhists call it. Followers also believe in the sacredness of life, compassion, service, reincarnation, and the laws of karma. We do not believe in violence or proselytizing."

"I always thought Hindus worship many gods," Jennifer said.

Stuart nodded, and Sri Bhattar said, "Many people think that, but actually, the statues you see in temple are manifestations of the one supreme God. Vedas emphatically assert that there is one God, who is described by wise men in different ways. Picture, if you will, an elephant surrounded by blind men. Each will describe the elephant differently, but it is the same elephant. Over four thousand years ago, ancient seers received what would be described as revelations while meditating. These sacred verses were passed along orally for thousands of years and were compiled by a sage named Krishna Dwaipayana Veda Vyasa. He compiled the first three books of what we call the Vedas: Rig, Yajur, and Sama. The fourth Veda, Atharva, is attributed to the sages Angiras and Atharvan.

"Hindus believe in the divine origin of the Vedas. They are considered to be without beginning and are eternal. Just as the law of gravitation existed before its discovery, it would exist even if all of humanity forgot what it was. Such are the spiritual truths in the Vedas. I'm getting to my point about the different manifestations for God. Throughout history, seekers and sages with different languages and cultures have understood God in their own way. Through various needs in hardship and plenty, God has been interpreted in different ways. There are four separate denominations of Hinduism. The power of God has manifested itself in separate gods and goddesses, with small g. All are different manifestations of the one supreme God. This is not unlike the Trinity in Christianity and the veneration given to Mary by the Catholic faith."

"Do you think the God of Christianity, Judaism, and Islam is the same God as Brahman?" Stuart asked.

"In Rig Veda, it is stated, 'Truth is one, sages call it by various names,'" the priest replied. "Hindus believe that all religions are pathways to God. This acceptance sets us apart from other religions in that the inclusive nature of Hinduism is a way to attain the harmony of all religions with God."

Sri Bhattar held his finger up. "'As the different streams having their sources in different places all mingled their water in the sea, so, O Lord, the different paths which men take through different tendencies, various thought they appear, all lead to Thee' is a well-known Hindu prayer."

"I thought the Bhagavad Gita was the holy book of Hinduism," Jennifer said.

"The Vedas are the revealed scripture," the priest replied. "The Upanishads are the knowledge texts of the Vedas. They explain the core philosophies of karma or the cumulative effects of one's actions, samsara or reincarnation, moksha or liberation of the soul, and the atman or the soul. The Brahma Sutra explains God's relation to the world and all beings. It also teaches how to attain the knowledge of God and spiritual liberation. The Bhagavad Gita is a practical truth, in that it combines Upanishads and Brahma Sutra in a manner easy to apply in daily living.

The Bhagavad Gita originally appeared as an episode in the *Mahabharat,* which is the largest epic poem in world literature. It contains more than one hundred thousand stanzas written by the great sage Vyasa. It was written in Sanskrit, and it has been transcribed into many languages, which are often accompanied by interpretations of their learned authors. Bhagavad Gita literally means song of God. The book is in the form of a dialogue between the incarnate god Krishna and a human hero named Prince Arjuna, who was on a battlefield before the start of a war. According to the Gita, an ideal person has devotion to God, rational discrimination, and selfless actions and meditates to attain the union of the soul to God."

"Tell me about your worship services," Stuart interrupted.

"Our temple is constantly busy with services or celebrations," the priest began. "Individuals or families can arrange special services to mark significant happenings in their lives. There is a worship service on Sundays that is open to the public. Our temple is always open to the public. It is quite a spectacular blend of colors, sounds, and smells. Priests chant scriptures, and prayers are recited. Food offerings are made. Incense is burned. There are times we have a visiting swami to give lectures on spirituality and philosophy. We have dances and dance instruction. There are times set aside for meditation and yoga."

"Are any of the services performed in English?" Jennifer asked.

"Only Sanskrit," the priest replied. "But there is always someone available to translate, should you like to visit."

"It all sounds rather complex," Jennifer said, smiling and waving to the retreating figure of the priest.

"That's why it takes many lifetimes to understand," Stuart said, chuckling.

TWENTY-SIX

Christianity, Part 2: The One Holy Catholic and Apostolic Church

Stuart Jones, Editor
(To be published Saturday, December 10, 2011)

When Jesus came to the region of Caesarea Philippi, he asked his disciples, "Who do people say the Son of Man is?" They replied, "Some say John the Baptist; others say Elijah; and still others, Jeremiah or one of the prophets." "But what about you?" he asked. "Who do you say I am?" Simon Peter answered, "You are the Messiah, the Son of the living God." Jesus replied, "Blessed are you, Simon, son of Jonah, for this was not revealed to you by flesh and blood, but by my Father in heaven. And I tell you that you are Peter, and on this rock, I will build my church, and the gates of Hades will not overcome it. I will give you the keys of the kingdom of heaven; whatever you bind on earth

will be bound in heaven, and whatever you loose
on earth will be loosed in heaven."
—Matthew 16:13–17

Christianity began following the death and resurrection of Jesus
Christ in the year AD 33, as mentioned in Part 1. Roman Catholics
comprise the largest group in the Christian faith. One in four
Christians are Catholics. The Catholic church is often referred to
as the mystical body of Christ because its members are united by
supernatural bonds to Christ and one another, as likened to a human
body. Christ is the head and founder of the church, unlike other
denominations that have human founders like Martin Luther or
John Calvin. Catholics believe in the Trinity and use the sign of the
Trinity to refer to God the Father, God the Son, and God the Holy
Spirit—one God in three parts. Another mystery of the church is
the immaculate conception that occurred in Mary, the mother of
Jesus. Sometimes she is referred to as the mother of the church. Early
bishops likened her to Eve, the mother of the living. Mary is the
mother of those living in Christ. She is often called upon in prayer
to be an advocate for those seeking answers and help.

Catholic worship is centered on the Eucharist, the receiving
of Christ's body and blood to transform the lives of believers. It is
required at minimum each year, but most commune weekly or daily
in order to live the good life that Christ intended, which is focused
on God, the Father, and which has the help of the Holy Spirit, who is
able to do good works. It is the duty of Catholics to live faithfully and
on a path that is pleasing to God. The term transubstantiation is used
to describe the transformation of wine and bread into the blood and
body of Christ. Jesus instituted this sacrament the night before his
arrest during Passover. Accounts of his sharing of wine and bread are
found in all four Gospels in the New Testament. For two thousand

years and around the world, priests administered the transformed substances at gatherings of believers in order that they might be one with Christ. It is yet another mystery, which is knowable only to God and not understandable by human reason alone.

The apostle Peter was the first successor of Christ, as directed by Christ himself when he told the then named disciple Simon in Matthew 16:18, "I say to you: You are Peter, and on this rock, I will build my church." After Christ's death and resurrection and during the beginnings of the early church, everyone looked to Peter for answers and decisions about how to proceed. He is thought to be the first pope in Rome in a papal line that extends to Pope Benedict today. The coming of the Holy Spirit upon the apostles at Pentecost signaled the beginning of Christianity in earnest. The early acts of the apostles, which is where the book of Acts in the New Testament gets its name, are what shaped the early Christian church into what it is two thousand years later.

Over the centuries, there have been two major schisms leading to the creation of Christian denominations apart from Catholicism. In 1054, the Greek-speaking Eastern Orthodox church separated from Latin-speaking Roman Catholics over two main doctrinal disagreements. The first was the role and authority of the pope. The second was over a clause in the Nicene Creed. The Eastern Orthodox believe that the Holy Spirit proceeded from only God the Father. The western Catholics believed that the Holy Spirit proceeded from the Father and the Son.

Five hundred years later, Protestant reformers disagreed with the pope and his allies over papal authority, the doctrine of salvation involving indulgences, and scriptural interpretation, among other things. Reformers believed that Christians should be able to read and hear the scriptures in their own languages. Protestant churches continued to evolve and break into new denominations, which continues even to this day. The Catholic churches of today are the remnant of the early Catholic church established by Christ through Peter and the other apostles.

The Catholic church claims that the true church of Christ must bear the four marks, holy (1), catholic (2), apostolic (3), and church (4). The Catholic church is one because all its members are united under one and the same visible head, the pope. Only the Catholic church possesses this mark of unity. Other denominations having only fragments of Christianity are divided in doctrine and practice, relying on no authority but the judgment of self-selected leaders. Other denominations reject the authority Christ imparted to Peter and his successors. The Catholic church is one in faith, one in worship, and one in recognizing the papal authority established by Christ. The Catholic church is holy because it was established by Christ, who was holy.

The doctrines that the church teaches are recognized as holy and have transformed the lives of saints, martyrs, and good Catholics throughout the centuries. There are bad Catholics who do not use the means of grace at their disposal, but Christ forewarned of them in his parables of the fishes in the net and the wheat and chaff. The Catholic church is universal, which is another term for catholic—with a small c. It is destined to last forever. The church today teaches the same doctrine it received from Christ. It reaches all races and places and sends its missionaries to the most remote places on Earth. The Catholic Charities organization is the largest nongovernmental provider of education and medical services in the world. Finally, the Catholic Church is apostolic because it was founded by Christ and given to the apostle Peter and the other apostles. The supreme power of Saint Peter in the church has been passed down through the unbroken line of his successors in Rome.

The Catholic church believes, as all Christian churches do, that there is life after death and that believers can be united with the saints and loved ones who have previously passed. However, salvation and the means of grace are not given without some relation to the divine institution established by Christ. Jesus is the ultimate advocate for the soul.

The archdiocese serves more than 2.5 million Catholics statewide and nearly 300 parishes in the greater metro area. Sunday is the traditional day of worship, and most parishes have more than one time for mass, making it easy for believers to worship. Visitors are always welcome; however, the Eucharist is administered only to baptized Catholics who are not in a state of mortal sin.

TWENTY-SEVEN

The Mother

Stuart's phone was ringing, but he was in the shower after his run. Jennifer saw that it was his Aunt Becky, so she answered it. "Hello, this is Jenny. Is this Aunt Becky?"

"Hello dear. Yes, this is me. Is Stuart available?" Becky said.

"He is in the shower. Can I have him call you back?" Jennifer asked.

"Well, I have bad news. Alice had a stroke and is in the hospital. They don't expect her to live much longer," Becky said.

"Oh no. I'm so sorry. Oh, this is terrible. Stuart wanted to tell his mother about the babies," Jennifer said.

"She knew from his messages," Becky said. "She was so proud and excited."

"What hospital is she in?" Jennifer asked. "We'll head there tonight."

"She is in Mercy Hospital," Becky said. "Please be careful. I'll meet you here."

Jennifer ended the phone call and went into the bathroom. She opened the shower door, and Stuart saw immediately that something was wrong.

"What is it?" he said in a panic.

"Stuart, it's not me," Jennifer said, coming into the shower to give him a hug. "It's your mom. Becky called to say that she had a stroke, and it is not good. She said she might not make it much longer."

Stuart turned off the water. "I need to get up there," he said.

"I'm coming with you, and you will not stop me," Jennifer said.

"I want you there," he said, holding her. "Come on. You're wet. Let's get changed."

Six hours later, Stuart parked in the lot of Mercy Hospital. He and Jennifer held hands as they walked through the emergency entrance.

"She's not in labor," Stuart said, holding his hand up to the nurse behind the desk. "I just need a wheelchair for her. We are here to see my mom, who had a stroke and isn't doing well. I hope we are not too late."

The clerk behind the desk brought a wheelchair around for Jennifer. "What is your mom's name?" she asked.

"Alice Jones," Stuart replied.

"I'll get the doctor for you," she said.

What seemed like an hour later, which was actually about four minutes later, a short, stocky man in a lab coat came through the door.

"Mr. Jones?" he queried.

"Yes?" Stuart said hopefully.

"I'm Dr. Sanders," the physician said somberly as he shook Stuart's hand.

"This is my wife Jennifer," Stuart replied.

"I'll take you to see your mother and aunt."

They went into the corridor, started making their way into the bowels of the hospital, and turned down one hallway and then another.

No wonder they made us wait at the desk, Jennifer thought as Stuart pushed her through the passageways in the wheelchair.

They came to a doorway and entered a dimly lit room with a single bed and a myriad of monitors blinking and beeping. A small woman looked up from the bedside and came around to give Stuart a hug.

"Hello, Aunt Becky," Stuart said, hugging her. "This is Jennifer, my wife."

"No, don't get up," Aunt Becky said as Jennifer tried to stand up. Becky leaned over and gave her a quick hug. "I'm so glad to meet you," she said. "Hello, Dr. Sanders." She held out her hand to shake his. Then everyone in the room turned to look at the once-vibrant body of Alice Jones.

"I'm afraid I don't have good news," Dr. Sanders said. "Her scans don't show any brain activity or response to stimulus. She is breathing on her own for now, but I don't think she'll improve. Your mother had a medical power of attorney assigned to her sister, Becky, and an advanced directive that no life-prolonging treatment be given in the event of brain damage. I think the stroke most likely occurred in the brain stem. The EEG studies on brain activity are very weak," Dr. Sanders said, showing a diagram of the brain to the group. "She is in a coma and will probably require life support soon if you want her heart to keep pumping. But that would go against her wishes," the doctor added gently.

"I didn't want to make any decision without you here, Stuart," Becky said, tearfully sniffing into a Kleenex.

"It's okay, Becky," he answered. "We both know she wouldn't want to live like this." Turning to Dr. Sanders he asked, "How much longer do you think she'll be like this?"

"It is doubtful she'll live through the night," he said grimly. "My condolences." After a brief pause, he said, "I have other patients to see now, but the ICU nurses are just out in the hall if you need anything at all."

"Can you turn this infernal noise off?" Stuart asked.

"Yes," Dr. Sanders responded. "Here is how you shut the sound off in case it automatically comes back on." He showed the group which button to push to turn the sound off. Now there were only lights and moving lines on the machines. "The nurses will come in if the heartbeat should go flat. They will probably check on you, though, before that happens," Dr. Sanders told them as he headed out the door.

Becky went around on the other side of the bed and sat back down in her chair. Stuart sat on his mom's bed and took her hand in his. Jennifer wheeled herself near the foot of the bed so she could look at her mother-in-law. *I wish I could have known her,* she thought.

"Mom," Stuart said gently, looking down at his mother's near-lifeless body, "I'm here. I brought Jennifer to meet you." His voice cracked. "What was she doing before the stroke?" he asked Becky.

"We were bowling," Becky replied. "We got back from California yesterday and decided to do something fun before going back to work tomorrow. She was just sitting there, and then she slumped over onto the floor." Becky resumed her crying into her Kleenex. After a while, she looked up at Stuart. "She was going to call you after bowling," she said tearfully. "I should have made her call you before we went. We heard all your wonderful messages on the answering machine."

"That's okay, Aunt Becky," Stuart said as he reached out for her hand. "I'm glad she was doing something fun. You know she never had time to do anything fun."

"She used to be like that," Becky answered, squeezing his hand. "After Bob died and she moved up here with me, we liked to do fun things. She was still a workaholic, but I could get her out of the house occasionally."

"You were really good for her," Stuart told her. "I'm sorry Uncle

Bob died, but I'm glad she had good company to live with. She was always nervous when I was around because she worried that I would ask her about my father. It was always a big elephant in the room for us."

"I know, honey," Becky said, squeezing his hand again. "I never could understand why she held that secret. She never told me or wanted to talk about it. I could tell it broke her heart. Our parents were awful to her. I think that might have been the reason she buried it forever. If it didn't exist, maybe they would forgive her."

"I existed though," Stuart said glumly.

"She loved you, Stuart," Becky said firmly. "She just didn't know how to show it. She was hurt, lonely, and heartbroken. I think that is why she worked all the time—so she didn't have time to dwell on how hurt she was."

"I'm thankful she let me spend so much time with Samil and his family," he said. He brightened and continued, "I saw them recently."

"That's wonderful," Becky responded. "I know how much your mom helped them after Samil died."

"She did?" Stuart asked. "I never knew that."

"They talked practically every day and encouraged each other because you were so down," she told him.

"I shouldn't have put myself into such a shell," Stuart said. "I guess I understand my mom a little better."

Jennifer wheeled over to Stuart's side and put her hand on his knee. He reached down and gave her a long hug and then wiped the tears out of his eyes as he sat up. They all turned to look at the door when they heard a gentle knocking sound. A priest came into the room and smiled at Aunt Becky.

"Father Connelly," Becky said as she shook his hand.

"Hello, Becky," he said. "This must be Stuart," he said, reaching out to shake his hand.

"Hello," Stuart said, looking first at Father Connelly and then quizzically at Aunt Becky.

"Stuart," Becky said, "this is our priest, Father Connelly. Father, this is Stuart, Alice's son and his wife, Jennifer."

"Hello," Father Connelly said to both of them. "I'm so sorry it took me this long to get here. I was in the city and came as soon as I could. Is there any improvement?"

"No, Father," Becky said. "She probably won't last through the night."

"May I perform the sacraments?" Father Connelly asked Becky.

"Yes, Father," Becky said, moving out of the way.

Stuart followed her to the foot of the bed and moved Jennifer's chair over to allow the priest more room. "I didn't know she was Catholic," he whispered to Aunt Becky.

"We were raised Catholic, Stuart," Becky whispered back. "We've been going to Father Connelly's parish church for a couple of years now."

"Alice talked of you often, Stuart," Father Connelly said. "Shall we bow our heads?"

Jennifer held Stuart's hand as Father Connelly administered the last rites to Alice. After the final prayer, he told Becky and Stuart that he would check with them in the morning in case any funeral arrangements needed to be discussed. Then he left.

Jennifer had been wanting to talk to Alice, and she finally got up her nerve. "Help me up, Stuart," she said, reaching up for him. She stood, turned, and sat next to Stuart. She picked up Alice's near-lifeless hand.

"Alice," Jennifer said, "I'm Jenny, Stuart's wife. It's nice to meet you." Jennifer thought, *I've always heard that hearing is the last to go, so here I go.* Jennifer placed Alice's hand on her swollen belly. "These are your grandchildren, Alice," she said. "There are seven. I sure wish you could be around when they are born. We could really use the help." Jennifer paused, looked at Stuart, and smiled. "I'm hopeful they will be all right, but a couple of the babies are two or three months behind the others due to a strange condition I have.

They may not make it. I know you will be there for them in heaven." Her voice cracked. "My mom will be there to help you with them if that happens. You'll like my mom. Her name is Naomi Carter," she added. She wasn't really certain how one met another in heaven.

"Jenny," Stuart said gently, squeezing her shoulder as tears slid down her cheeks.

"Stuart," Jennifer said, looking up at him. "Maybe this is another God thing—taking your mom so she can look after the babies in heaven."

"Jennifer," Stuart said firmly, "nothing is going to happen to our babies. They will be just fine. Stop worrying. It's not good for you or them."

"I'll help," Aunt Becky said. "I would love to help rock them and change diapers. I don't have any grandchildren yet. It will be good practice."

Stuart and Jennifer laughed. and all three looked at Alice. It was like she wasn't there. The monitor was flatlining.

"Does it look like she is smiling to you?" Stuart asked.

"It seems like there is a glow about her," Becky said.

"She is in heaven," Jennifer said.

The door opened, and a nurse walked in.

Five days later, they were at Aunt Becky's table going through papers and files and trying to find Alice's will.

"I know she just had it updated to include you, Jennifer," Becky said.

"We'll have to call the attorney tomorrow, Becky," Stuart said. "Do you remember the name?"

"Yes," Becky answered. "We used the same one. I've got a card here somewhere."

"Are you sure you don't want us to get a hotel room?" Jennifer asked. "I feel bad your kids had to stay with friends when they came for the funeral."

"They would stay with their friends anyway," Becky said. "Wrong generation!" she said pointing at herself. "It was nice to meet your dad and your coworkers."

"It was so nice that everyone came!" Jennifer exclaimed.

"I was sure shocked," Stuart chimed in.

Jennifer opened what she thought was a ledger, but it turned out to be a scrapbook. She began to peruse the pages and stopped. "Stuart," she said.

"Hmmm," he absently replied.

"What's your middle name?" she asked. "I'm embarrassed to even ask that," she told Aunt Becky.

"Jonathan," was his reply.

"I think I know who your father is," she said, holding out the book.

Stuart raced over and grabbed the book from Jennifer. He looked at the page she held open and then at the next few pages. He absentmindedly sat down on Aunt Becky's cat, which screeched and bounded away.

"Jonathan Stuart, MD, specialist in multiple and problem pregnancies announces the opening of his obstetric practice in Toronto, Ontario on July 1, 1990." He looked up. "She named me after him," he told them. He continued perusing the pages.

"That's got to be him," Jennifer concurred. "Do you suppose she looked him up on the computer once the internet was available?"

"You look a lot like him, Stuart," Aunt Becky said, looking at the picture in the book.

"Oh, geez," Stuart said, running his hand through his hair.

"What?" Becky and Jennifer said in unison.

"His oldest son just died," Stuart said. "He presumably died in Afghanistan, but they haven't been able to recover the bodies from the helicopter crash." Stuart looked at his watch for the date. "That was two weeks ago. She must have just added this article the day she got back from California."

"Stuart, he looks just like you," Jennifer said.

"What's that called?" Becky asked. "Someone in the world who looks just like you?"

"Doppelganger," Stuart said numbly. "But I don't think it counts if you're related."

"We have to go see him," Jennifer said.

TWENTY-EIGHT

The Father

The drive to the Toronto address, which Jennifer had found on the internet, was only two-and-a-half hours away. At ten in the morning, they pulled up in front of a two-story, stately brick home with Christmas wreaths in every window. Jennifer had lain down in the back seat with her legs up over the passenger seat, which had been pushed forward all the way. It took Stuart a couple of tries to extricate her from the car. They walked up to the front door—or waddled in Jennifer's case.

"I'm afraid to knock," Stuart said as they stood at the front door.

"Well, I have to use the bathroom, so one of us is going to have to knock soon," Jennifer announced.

Just as Stuart was getting ready to knock, the door opened, and a teenage girl stood there with a surprised look on her face. "Michael?" she asked. Then turning, she screamed, "Michael's here!"

Stuart put his hands up. "No, I'm not Michael. I'm his half-brother."

The girl had already run away from the door, and a distinguished couple came from a door in the back of the foyer and stopped when they saw Stuart.

Before anyone else jumped to the wrong conclusion, Stuart announced quickly, "I'm Stuart Jones, Alice Jones's son."

"My God," the man said. "You look exactly like our son Michael. We just buried him this morning."

"Jon," the woman said, "was Alice the high-school sweetheart you told me about?" Coming forward to embrace Stuart and Jennifer, she said, "I'm Cassandra Stuart. Please call me Cassie. This is Jonathan, whom I assume is your father?"

"I had no idea!" Jonathan exclaimed. "I ... I ... I just don't know what to say."

Gesturing to Jennifer and her swollen belly, Stuart asked, "Could we please sit down somewhere?"

"Of course, please come in," Jonathan said, snapping out of his surprised stupor. "You must be due any minute now," he told Jennifer as he helped her to a chair in the sitting room.

"I'm only five-and-a-half months, and I really need to go to the bathroom first," she told him.

Cassie spoke up. "Jennifer, come with me. The nearest bathroom is just down the hall."

She could hear Stuart and his father discussing her pregnancy as she walked down the hall. She stopped to look at the pictures hanging on the wall. It was amazing how much Stuart looked like his half-brother. As she reappeared, both men stopped to look at her. They jumped up to help her sit on the couch. She lay back into the pillows. Stuart removed her shoes, and Jonathan put her feet up on the footrest.

"Thank you," she told them. "I know it is important to rest. Did Stuart tell you that the babies are at different gestational ages?"

"Yes," Jonathan answered. "I am overwhelmed to discover that I have another son and am about to have seven grandchildren!"

Cassie returned with coffee and cookies. "I thought you all might like some refreshments before we discuss ... did I hear you say seven grandchildren?" she asked Jonathan. She looked wide-eyed at her husband, then Stuart, and finally Jennifer.

Just then, the door banged open, and the young teenager who had answered the door entered with three of her friends. "See," she said pointing at Stuart, "Michael is alive."

"I think I might need something stronger than coffee," Cassie said, putting the tray down on the ottoman.

Stuart rose and walked over to the teenager. "I wish I could be Michael for you," he said, "but I'm Stuart Jonathan Jones, your half-brother."

Jonathan came over and put his arm around the girl. "This is Caroline, our daughter," he told Stuart and Jennifer. "And this is Margot, Abby, and Lisa," he said, gesturing to the three girls standing beside Caroline. "Why don't you girls go get pizza," he said, pulling out his wallet.

"Dad," Caroline said, "it's not even lunchtime yet. And there's no way I'm staying out of this conversation."

"Caro," Cassie said sternly.

"That's okay, Mrs. Stuart," the one named Margot said. "We'll leave now." The girls turned and left.

"I'll tell them everything tomorrow anyway," Caro said, flopping down next to Jennifer on the couch. Cassie looked at Jennifer and smiled. "See what you have to look forward to?"

For the rest of the day, the teenager, the parents, and the parents-to-be sat in the living room and pieced together the life stories of Jonathan, Alice, Cassie, Michael, Caro, Stuart, Jennifer, and the babies. They cried when Jonathan told them how he had tried to find Alice when he returned from the war. They laughed when Cassie told them she had tried to make herself look like Alice so that Jonathan would ask her out. She, too, lost a loved one, whom she discovered had died in the war. They had met in a wartime locator office where people could go to seek information on lost loved ones.

Retelling stories of Michael and Caro made them laugh and cry again, but it seemed to lessen the pain of losing Michael.

"He was doing something he believed in," Jonathan said. "I'm so proud of him."

"Can I help with the babies?" Caro said.

TWENTY-NINE

The Hospital

Once the time neared midnight, Stuart and Jenny were persuaded to stay the night. Extra toothbrushes and pajamas were located. A muumuu costume, which was found in Caro's old dress-up box, was given to Jennifer. Stuart heard her get up for the second time that night to go to the bathroom. The sound of something crashing to the floor made him bolt out of bed. *Jennifer must have knocked the lamp over,* he thought.

"Stuart!" Jennifer cried as she sat down on the side of the bed. "I have a terrible headache, and I can't see."

She slumped over and Stuart tried to arouse her. "Jennifer! Jenny!" he yelled as he shook her shoulders. He raced out of the room and called for Jonathan.

A door opened at the other end of the house, and Jonathan appeared. "What is it, son? Jonathan asked.

"It's Jenny," Stuart said, grabbing his arm to head back to their room.

"Cassie, call 911," Jonathan called to her. "Tell me what happened," he said to Stuart. They reached Jennifer, who was still unresponsive.

"She said she had a severe headache and that she couldn't see," Stuart said.

Jonathan raced out of the room and shouted for Cassie to tell EMS that they might be dealing with a preeclamptic coma in a twenty-three-week pregnancy with multiple fetuses. He found his doctor's bag and raced back to Jennifer.

"I wish I had an IV set up," he told Stuart. "I'm going to give her an injection of magnesium sulfate, which may help to bring her blood pressure down. I suspect it is too high."

"Will it hurt the babies?" Stuart asked.

"The injection won't," Jonathan said. "We need to get her to hospital, start an IV, and run some tests. Her pulse is high."

"They're here," Cassie yelled down the hall.

Moments later, two paramedics came into the room with a gurney.

"I'm Dr. Stuart," Jonathan announced. "I just gave her 250 milligrams of mag sulfate. It is imperative we get her to the hospital fast. Can you load her up and start the IV in the ambulance?"

"Yes, sir," the closest attendant said.

"I'll ride along if that's okay," Jonathan stated rather than asked. "My specialty is problem pregnancies, and it now seems we have a problem."

"Can I go too?" Stuart asked.

Cassie spoke up. "Come with me Stuart. We'll follow behind, and I can drop you at the ER entrance."

Riding to the hospital was a nightmare. It seemed that every light turned red on purpose. The ambulance was well ahead of them by the time they reached the hospital.

"I know the way," Cassie reassured him. "Stuart, you need to be ready to make a decision about the babies."

"What do you mean?" he asked.

"Jon might need to do an emergency C-section to save Jennifer's life," Cassie said. "They have a great neonatal ICU here, though. We need to start praying now." Cassie pulled up beside the ambulance, and Stuart bolted out the door before she stopped.

Dr. Stuart was barking orders as they went down the hall to first ER bay. Residents and nurses were racing around. Jennifer had an IV in her hand, and she was soon hooked up to five monitors. Stuart could only think of his mom's bedside a few days earlier. His eyes filled with tears.

"Stuart," Jonathan said as he was looking at the fetal monitor. "I'm going to call in the surgical team just in case she doesn't respond to the IV and meds. I'm going to make arrangements with the neonatal unit. They've dealt with seven neonates before but not from the same mother."

Stuart could only shake his head. He was afraid that if he tried to speak, he would start crying and never stop. The room cleared out of personnel except for one nurse, who was looking at the monitors and wire hookups.

"Do you hear that?" she asked. "That's the babies."

Stuart heard several whooshes and felt a little reassured. He knelt down by Jennifer and took her hand.

"I'll get you a chair," the nurse said. "Talk to her. She will probably hear you or register your voice."

Stuart kissed her hand and leaned his head against her abdomen. "Please God," he pleaded, "don't let her die. I'm sorry that I gave up on you. Don't take her or the babies. I'm sorry. Forgive me. Jesus, please help her. I want to believe in you, Father." His voice broke, and he sobbed. "Father, Father, *Father*! Oh God, Henry!" Stuart fumbled for his cell phone and dialed Henry's number. His hand shook so badly that he had to try twice. Finally, it was ringing.

"Stuart, what's wrong?" barked Henry Carter so loudly that probably everyone in the ER heard him.

"Henry, Jennifer is in a coma," Stuart sobbed. "They might have to take the babies."

"Put me on speaker," Henry directed. "Can she hear me?"

"Yes," Stuart answered.

"Jenny," Henry said calmly, "it's your dad, honey. You come on around now. Your mother said it's not time. She wanted me to tell you that. I know you think I'm crazy for talking to your mother, but I hear her voice in my head—not all the time but just when I think about you. Just a few minutes ago, I heard her say, *Tell Jennifer it's not time yet.* I thought she was talking about having the babies, but I think she meant it's not time for you to die. Jenny, honey, wake up." Stuart rested his head on their clasped hands and continued to pray silently.

"Daddy?" Jennifer's weak voice sounded amidst all the beeps and whooshes.

Stuart's head shot up, and he called for the nurse. "Henry," he said into the phone, "did you hear that?"

"Stuart?" Jennifer coughed. "What happened?"

She started to sit up, but Stuart held her shoulders down. "Jen, you fainted just after you said you had a bad headache. You are in the hospital. They might have to deliver the babies."

"No!" Jennifer opened her eyes. "It's not time," she said.

"Jenny," Henry spoke through the speaker, "let the doctors do what is best for you and the babies."

"They have a really good neonatal unit here, Jen," Stuart told her. "You need to relax and bring your blood pressure down."

"I feel better, Stuart," she said. "I don't have the headache anymore. Really, I feel so much better."

Dr. Stuart came around through the doorway. "Thank God!" he exclaimed. Looking at the monitor, he continued, "Your pressure is normal, and your heart rate is slowing. The babies sound good. I ordered ultrasound to come, so we can have a look at them."

"You won't take them now?" Jennifer asked.

"Not if you continue to improve," he answered. "I think it might be a good idea to admit you, so you can get complete bed rest. That will buy at least four-to-six more weeks for them."

"Stuart," Jennifer said and turned to him, "will our insurance cover this?"

"It damn well better," Henry Carter barked through the phone. Everyone jumped and then laughed. "If it doesn't, I'll pay for it. I'm heading out the door now. I'll see you in a few hours."

"Daddy, drive safely," Jennifer told him, but he had already disconnected.

Stuart pocketed his phone and sat down. He rubbed his face with his hands and felt himself start to tear up again. Jennifer reached for his hands and held them. They looked at each other and smiled through their tears.

"Stuart," Jennifer said softly. "I had the strangest dream, or maybe it wasn't a dream. I saw my mom, and I saw your mom. They were smiling. My mom said I couldn't stay. I saw you, too, or I thought it was you. Oh…, it was Michael!" She looked at Jonathan.

"Did my heart stop in the ambulance?" Jennifer asked.

"It was a wild ride," Dr. Stuart answered. "We thought it was the monitor acting up. We never had to do chest compressions. It started working correctly just as we drove up to the building." The door opened, and an X-ray tech entered the room with the portable ultrasound machine.

"Okay," Dr. Stuart said eagerly, "Let me see these grandchildren of mine."

THIRTY

Hinduism: A Way of Life

Stuart Jones, Editor, and Abe Hoffman, Staff Writer
(To be published January 13, 2012)

> Never was there a time when I did not exist, nor
> you, nor all these kings; nor in the future shall any
> of us cease to be.
> —The Bhagavad Gita, 2.12

> For those who see Me everywhere and see all things
> in Me, I am never lost, nor are they ever lost to Me.
> —The Bhagavad Gita 6.30

Hinduism was coined by the British during the Colonial era to describe the religious and cultural traditions of the people living in the region known as Hindustan. The correct term for this religion is Sanatana Dharma, which means forever duty, encompassing devotion to God, attaining knowledge of true self, and selfless actions, all with the goal of achieving liberation of the soul (moksha). It is the world's oldest religion and the third most followed around the globe. One

135

common misconception of Hinduism is that they worship multiple gods. Hindus believe in and worship one God. The various statues in the temples are different manifestations of the same God. It is similar to the various statues of Christ and worship of the Trinity in Christianity. Sages of millennia past received revelations from God, which have been passed down throughout the eons and finally recorded in sacred scripture called the Vedas. The truths recorded in the Vedas are considered to be without beginning, for they contain eternal truths. It is of interest to note that Buddhism, Jainism, and Sikhism are thought to have evolved from Hinduism.

The basic beliefs of Hinduism can be summarized as follows:

1. The divinity of the soul means that God is omnipresent, and every human soul is divine. The goal of human life is to be at one with God through the practice of meditation or yoga.
2. The unity of all existence means that in the ever-changing world of cause and effect, God is the only eternal and unchanging reality. Behind all names and forms, there is only one reality (Brahman).
3. The harmony of religions means that all religions are pathways to the same goal. This belief shows the universal and inclusive nature of Hinduism and a way to attain religious harmony.

For followers of Sanatana Dharma, religion, rituals, and spirituality are a way of life. They do not separate religion from any other activity they experience. Children begin to learn early on the importance of spirituality. They gradually learn to focus on rituals and beliefs at temple gatherings. The learning is gradual. One does not teach calculus to kindergarten students, but they can learn math basics. The same can be said for Hinduism. The rituals and festivals are an important way to connect with the divine and are the initial building blocks that lead to a personal spiritual journey.

Some of the key elements of Sanatana Dharma include the belief in selfless action (karma) and a moral law that governs actions (dharma), attaining the means and resources to lead a meaningful life (artha), and pursuing the ultimate goal of human life—liberation of the soul (moksha). Going on a spiritual journey requires a balance in regard to ritual practices. Meditation and yoga are balanced with understanding the meaning behind the rituals, seeking guidance from a religious leader, and attending study groups. Hindu temples are places of friendship, learning, culinary delights, dance instruction, Sanskrit instruction, and individual and group worship opportunities. One does not have to be a member to seek help in the practice of yoga or meditation.

"Om," the universal symbol and sound of meditation, is defined by Hindu scripture as being the primordial sound of creation. It is the original vibration of the universe. From this first vibration, all other vibrations are able to manifest. As yogis commonly conclude their meditations with the chanting of "Om," the Judeo-Christian utterance of "Amen" and the Islamic version, "*Amin*," are used by followers to signal the Divine at the end of a prayer. Om encompasses all of creation, and its energy can be attained by anyone who seeks it, regardless of their faith.

There are at least two hundred temples or places of Hindu worship in the greater metro area. There is more than one denomination, so you have many choices in finding a temple where you feel most at home.

THIRTY-ONE

The Family

"I think you should keep the appointment, Stuart," Jennifer said the next morning. "I'm being well taken care of here. Cassie, Caro, and your father will keep me company." She smiled when she said, "Your father."

"I don't want to leave you in case anything else happens," Stuart said, kissing her hand.

"You're only a couple of hours away," she replied. "Go and see what the attorney has to say about your mom's will and finish helping Aunt Becky clean out her things."

Stuart reached down and gave Jennifer a slow, hungry kiss. He reluctantly stopped when he heard a knock at the door.

"Daddy!" Jennifer exclaimed as Henry entered the room.

"Hi, honey," Henry said as he reached down to give her a hug. He stood up and shook Stuart's hand. "How are you, Stuart?" Henry asked.

"Fine. How about you?" Stuart asked.

"Hello," Jonathan said as he came around the door. "How is everyone?"

Stuart made the introductions, and Jonathan and Henry hit it off immediately. They left after a while to go to lunch. Stuart decided to take off for his meeting with his mom's attorney, and Jennifer snuggled down for a nap.

It was about midnight when Stuart slipped quietly back into Jennifer's room. He kissed her on the forehead and sat down to watch her sleep. His mind was racing, and he knew sleep wouldn't come if he tried. Aunt Becky had everything boxed up and said she would arrange for his mom's things to be donated. He had four boxes of his mother's personal items, pictures, and papers along with mementos he thought Jennifer would like in the trunk and back seat of his car. He still couldn't believe what the attorney had revealed about his mother's estate. He knew his mom so little. He felt guilty that he didn't have a closer relationship with her, but she worked all the time. Now it all made sense. He wished with all his might that he could talk with her again. He remembered what Jennifer had said about seeing her. *Jesus, I really want to see her again someday. Help me believe. Forgive me,* Stuart prayed silently. Then he fell asleep.

Six weeks later, Stuart was in the hallway talking to Abe. "Thanks, Abe, for putting the finishing touches on the Hindu article and the February article on major religious sites," Stuart told him.

"My pleasure," Abe replied. "I didn't have to add much. The conversation and notes you took were very helpful, and the religious sites' article was pulled out of the morgue. Mrs. B. said to tell you we have our own page now. I think at last count we had 330 or 340 signed up for our church listing."

"That's great, Abe," Stuart said, smiling. "Jennifer will be so pleased with that news."

"How is she?" Abe asked.

"Doing really well, and so are the babies," Stuart answered.

"Give her my love," Abe said. "Everyone here says hi and sends their love."

"Listen, Abe," Stuart said in a more serious tone. "I'm going to write one more column for next month. I already turned in my notice to Henry. I want to be there to tell all of you together, but Jennifer could have the babies any day now, and I don't want to leave her."

"Actually, we were discussing that just this morning," Abe said. "You are about to be a very busy man."

"How in the world did you know?" Stuart asked incredulously.

"It isn't ESP," Abe said, laughing. "Jennifer has been keeping Mrs. B. updated."

"Things have really worked out," Stuart said. "The fortune my mom left me will get us through the next couple of years without me having to work. We are still working out where to live after the babies are born."

"All good problems to have," Abe said. "Instead of a good thing, I'd even say it's a God thing."

"Jennifer said that too," Stuart said, smiling. "Say hi to everyone for me."

Later, Stuart walked back into Jennifer's room and found her sitting on the bedside commode.

"Hey, you," he said. "You should have called me to help you."

"Stuart," Jennifer said, "I can stand up by myself. How's Abe?"

"Fine," Stuart answered. "He already knew I was leaving, of course."

Jennifer chuckled, "I told Mrs. B. yesterday when she called. He really isn't a mind reader." She started to stand up, and Stuart raced around to help her. She turned to give him a hug and kiss. "Thank you," she said. "I am so … oh!" Fluid was running down her leg and puddling on the floor. "I think my water broke."

Stuart reached over and pressed the call button. "Here, sit down."

He helped her sit back down on the commode. The nurse entered the room, followed by Dr. Stuart.

"I think my water broke," Jennifer said, pointing to the puddle on the floor.

"Well, I think it's time we met these boys and girls," Jonathan said. "I've had the neonatal unit and surgery team on notice for the past three weeks." He gave instructions to the nurse and then turned back to Jennifer and Stuart. "Are you feeling all right, Jennifer?" he asked

"I feel great," Jennifer replied. "Well, except for the eighty pounds I gained."

"You did it for the team," Jonathan said, smiling. The nurse returned with a wheelchair, and Stuart helped Jennifer perform the transfer. Then they were off to the delivery room.

"Are you still okay for the epidural?" Dr. Stuart asked Jennifer. "I'm glad you signed all the consents already."

"Yes," she replied. "I can be awake when you perform the C-section, right?"

"Right," he answered. "But remember that we might have to convert to general in the event of excessive bleeding or an unforeseen complication."

"I know," Jennifer said. "Oh, Stuart, would you call my dad?

"I just sent him a text and told him I would keep him updated," Stuart said, squeezing her hand and then looking at his buzzing phone. "He said he would let your mom know."

"Stuart," Jonathan said. "Come with me, and I'll show you where you can change into scrubs."

Jennifer was helped onto the delivery table by a nurse, who said her name was Anna. Soon there were sounds of monitors and the familiar whooshes of the babies' hearts as she was hooked up to the leads. They taped them to her chest and abdomen. Jennifer noticed the four enclosed bassinets and started to panic, but then she remembered they were going to put more than one baby in the cribs.

"I'm not scared," she blurted out just as Stuart and his father walked into the delivery room. Stuart reached for her hands.

"That's right, Jenny," Dr. Stuart said calmly. "Stay calm, you're doing so well. Stuart, you can stand here next to the bed. If you feel faint, sit down in this chair."

There were at least eight nurses, techs, and assistants moving about the room. They were opening packs, adjusting equipment, and moving rolling carts. Three doctors came into the room and introduced themselves. The pediatricians and Dr. Stuart went out to the scrub room. The anesthesiologist busied himself getting ready to start the epidural.

"Jennifer, can you sit up?" the anesthesiologist asked.

"Yes, if Stuart helps me," she replied. She leaned against Stuart as the needle was inserted into her lower back.

"There," the anesthesiologist said. It should start taking effect in about fifteen to thirty minutes. You will feel numb from your lower ribs down.

Dr. Stuart returned with his hands in surgical gloves. He was wearing a mask like everyone else, but Jennifer could tell he was smiling. "We'll wait until you are good and numb," he said. "You will feel some tugging and pressure, but you shouldn't feel pain. You'll let me know if something feels painful, okay? You can watch what is happening on the mirror above."

"Oh good," she said happily. "I wasn't sure if I was going to be able to see anything with all these drapes over me."

"Stuart, you can watch up there too," Jonathan told him. "Just stay there because there will be lots of moving people, and it is crucial they move as quickly as possible."

"How will we know which one is which after they are born?" Stuart asked.

"A nurse will write a number on their heels with a Sharpie," he said. "Once they are all out, assessed, and cleaned up, you can decide how you want to distinguish between them. We will have our multiple births' coordinator reach out to you by the end of the week."

"Gosh, you think of everything," Stuart said.

"Let's hope so," Dr. Stuart replied. "Time out!" he barked.

All in all, getting the babies out was over in fifteen minutes. Jennifer still felt tugging and pulling. They were finally sewing her up. She would never forget seeing the little ones as they came out of her womb. They were such tiny things.

"Let's call him Adam," Stuart said of their firstborn.

He only weighed 680 grams. She would have to do the calculations to convert to pounds and ounces. Baby number two weighed 1,021 grams.

"Can we call her Naomi?" Jennifer asked.

"Certainly," Stuart replied, kissing her forehead.

Baby number three weighed 1,077 grams.

"Alice," they both said in unison as the wriggling little girl was whisked away. Baby number four weighed in at 1,361 grams.

"Let's call him Henry," Stuart said softly.

"Or Jonathan?" Jennifer asked.

"Chances are there will be another boy, so let's stick with Henry, or I will never be able to face your father again," Stuart said, laughing quietly.

Baby number five weighed 1,588 grams.

"Welcome to the world Jonathan Michael Jones," Jennifer said and noticed that Jonathan was blinking rapidly. She squeezed Stuart's hand. "Oh look, Stuart, they're holding hands!" Jennifer squealed as baby number six wouldn't leave the womb without number seven. They immediately started squalling when the nurse unclasped their hands.

"Better put those two in the same incubator," Jonathan said, looking relieved. A nurse was wiping his brow, and his eyes with a blue towel.

"Would it be okay if we called the boy Sami?" Stuart asked Jennifer.

"Only if we call the little girl Yara," Jennifer responded quickly.

"Thank you, Jenny," Stuart said. His voice cracked. Tears were filling his eyes, which made Jennifer start to cry. He kissed her gently, mixing their tears together cheek to cheek.

"How much did baby six and seven weigh?" Jennifer asked.

"They were 2,325 and 2,438 respectively," a nurse replied from behind the last bassinet. Stuart and Jennifer's eyes met in understanding.

"I'm glad the first delivery was a girl," Jennifer told Stuart.

"Jenny, it doesn't matter," Stuart said and kissed her again.

"Can I hold one?" Jennifer asked.

"Let me get you fixed up," Jonathan told her. "Then we'll wheel you down to the NICU, and you can hold to your delight. The last bassinet was wheeled out the door.

The pediatrician called Dr. Jensen stayed behind. "It really is quite remarkable," Dr. Jensen said. "All the babies scored normal on their APGAR scores. Baby Adam is borderline. The littlest ones will need to remain in the NICU until their breathing is more stable. The last two we will keep overnight or maybe a couple of days, but I think you can take them home in a few days."

"Oh, that's wonderful!" Jennifer said enthusiastically. "Thank you, doctor. Stuart, what are you doing?"

"I'm texting your dad," he replied. Then turning to Dr. Jensen, he said, "Thank you so much."

"I'll give you follow-up instructions at the time of discharge," the doctor informed them. "Congratulations, it really is quite miraculous."

THIRTY-TWO
Inside Religion Revisited

Stuart Jones, Past Editor
(To be published March 9, 2012)

Hello, readers,

Nine months ago, if you would have told me I wouldn't be the religion editor any longer, I wouldn't have believed you. Nine months ago, I wrote that I was not a religious person, but miracles have a way of changing one's outlook and turning even the hardest agnostic into a believer. I have journeyed with you inside the religions of our beloved city. I can safely affirm my rediscovered belief in God, his infinite love for us, and his desire to have a relationship with each of us. I am still learning about my newfound religion. For the sake of not disappointing anyone, I will keep my choice of religion to myself. However, I do believe in miracles and the profound peace that comes in the presence of the Divine.

Over the past nine months, I have made peace with my best friend's death, lost a mother, found a father, found a wife and soulmate, became a father to seven—yes, seven beautiful babies—and was blessed with the means to support them without employment in the near future. If that isn't good karma, I don't know what is. I also believe that religion is firmly implanted in the hearts of all people even though they have not received direct revelation from God.

I know that sales of the newspaper have gone up, in part, thanks to our efforts to inform you about religious opportunities in the city. It is still my hope that this knowledge of religion without political bias will enlighten and encourage you to seek out a faith family of your own. You will find it hard to fight life's battles without the spiritual intervention of the Divine and help from like-minded friends. I leave future columns in the very capable hands of Abe Hoffman and Edith Jeffery, who may or may not require a new editor. I want to thank both of them for their commitment and expertise in writing articles that you, the reader, are interested in reading. A sincere thanks goes to my father-in-law, Henry Carter, for hiring me in the first place, but more importantly, for introducing me to his beautiful daughter, Jennifer. I am considering starting a blog of my hectic life as the father of seven. If I do, I will be sure to let you know where to find me. In the meantime, it is still my hope that you will gain a unique understanding of your religion and the religion of others and will live by the golden rule.

EPILOGUE

Six Years and Six Months Later

They're having fun, she thought as she put the last of the dishes from the Fourth of July party into the dishwasher. Stuart and the children were having a squirt gun war. The squirt guns were a gift from Grandpa Henry, who had just left before getting soaked. It was a wonderful dinner. Henry, Jonathan, Cassie, Caro, Yara, Ahmed, Amina, and her boyfriend were there surrounding them with their love. The sun was low in the west. *I'm so tired,* she thought and lay down on the porch hammock to shut her eyes. She could hear the children yelling at one another and their dad in Arabic. She was so happy that they were bilingual. She and Stuart determined in the hospital that he would speak only Arabic and that she would speak only English so that they would learn both languages. Yara and Ahmed helped reinforce the Arabic, and Henry, Jonathan, Cassie, and Caro helped reinforce the English. She was drifting into sleep.

"*Fa ʿala thalika al ʾāna.*" Sammi was just about to squirt her with his gun. The children were egging him on telling him, "Do it now," in Arabic. As she heard the chanting, she suddenly had a view of her attacker appear in her sleep. "*Fa ʿala thalika al ʾāna. Fa ʿala thalika al ʾāna.*" Jennifer saw her attacker's face. He was frightened and scared. He didn't want to rape her. She knew it by the look on his face. "*Fa ʿala thalika al ʾāna.*"

"Stuart!" she screamed as the cold water hit her legs and abdomen.

"Sammi, stop!" Stuart scolded. "Jennifer, what is it?" he asked as he knelt down.

"What were they saying?" she asked. "What were the children saying?"

"They were telling Sammi to spray you with the water gun," Stuart answered.

"No," Jennifer stopped him. "The phrase they used, what did it mean?"

"Do it," Stuart said. "They wanted him to spray you."

"Children, go get some popsicles," Jennifer said, dismissing them. They ran off with shouts of happiness. "That's what the terrorists were saying to my attacker," she said. "Stuart, I don't think he wanted to rape me. I just saw his face again when I heard the children shouting, and he was scared. I remember it vividly. They were shouting something else at him. Something like 'taqtala tuka.'"

Stuart thought about it for a moment. "Did it sound like 'âf'alhâ al'âna aw taqtala â'ilatuka?'"

"Yes!" she exclaimed. "What does it mean?"

"They were telling the man to do it, or they'd kill his family," Stuart answered.

"Oh, Stuart," Jennifer said dismally. "He didn't want to do it. He was as much a victim as I was." She sat back down in the hammock but then stood up again rapidly. "Stuart," she said, grabbing his arms. "We have his DNA! Can we find out who he was and let his family know?" she asked.

"I don't know, Jenny," he answered. "That was a long time ago. I can see if Jo Jo can find out anything."

"Please, oh, please do, Stuart," she pleaded.

"Come on," he said, giving her a hug. "Let's get the kids to bed, and I'll make some calls."

A week later, Stuart received a call on his cell phone and gave Jennifer a thumbs-up as he was listening. After he hung up, he said, "His name was Mohammed Mir, and he was only eighteen. His parents still live in Mecca."

"Stuart, we have to let them know what happened to him," Jennifer pleaded. "Can you go there and let them know?"

Stuart thought for a long time before answering. "What if we all go?" he asked. "Make it a cultural visit for the kids. They're old enough to behave, and they would like to see Mecca and the museum."

"Your imam friend isn't there anymore, is he?" Jennifer asked.

"No," Stuart replied. "He is somewhere in the Middle East—Dubai, I think." Jennifer held her head in her hands and shook it from side to side. "Jennifer, what happened to you will not happen again." Stuart tried to reassure her. "It isn't Ramadan. There won't be as many people around. We can see if Jo Jo and Big Dan will come provide security."

"They weren't much good the last time," she remarked dryly, looking up at him.

"I'll ask Yara and Ahmed if they'll come with us—our treat," he added. "It will be good for the kids to be in an Arabic country and use their Arabic."

"Well," she began, and then seeing his eyes so lit up and alive, she said, "Okay." He picked her up and swung her around and around until they were both dizzy.

"What are you doing, Papa?" Adam asked, coming outside with his half-eaten popsicle.

"We're going on a plane ride to Saudi Arabia!" Stuart shouted, letting Jenny fall back on the hammock. He picked up Adam and swung him around.

They approached the small house hesitantly. No one was on the street. The city was quiet as the sun started to set in the west. Stuart knocked lightly. Jennifer rolled her eyes and went forward to knock forcefully. "Bang, bang, bang," the sound echoed. It opened slightly, and two pairs of eyes peered out from the slit in the door.

"We come in peace," Stuart said in Arabic.

The door opened to reveal a slight woman and her child of about six or seven. Her husband appeared with a near identical twin of the child at the door. Soon, all were standing in the entryway and looking quizzically at one another. "Hello," Stuart said in Arabic. "We are looking for the parents of Mohammed Mir."

The woman cried and put her hand on her heart as her husband came to console her. "We are his parents," the man said in Arabic. "Do you know where he is?"

"Stuart," Jennifer interrupted. "They look exactly like Sammi and Yara," she said, gesturing to the twins.

Stuart looked at the twins and thought that they indeed looked like his oldest two children. Then it occurred to him that Sammi and Yara could be twins. "My name is Stuart Jones," he said in Arabic to the anxious couple. "And this is my wife, Jennifer." Jennifer smiled and bowed, offering the bread she had brought as a gift to the Mirs. "I'm sorry to inform you that your son was killed in a rescue attempt of a hostage six years ago," Stuart explained.

The Mirs looked crestfallen. Mrs. Mir had to finally sit down after attempting to hold in her tears. "We were afraid that was the case," Mr. Mir explained. "Mohammed was a good boy, but he was angry that the Taliban had kidnapped his sister and killed her. He vowed to find the men who violated her and promised us that he would kill them. It was a much different time then. The government has shut down these terrorist groups."

"Are these your children?" Stuart asked, gesturing to the look-alikes.

"Yes," Mrs. Mir explained. "I became pregnant about six years ago after Mohammed disappeared. Twins run in our family. This is my second set of twins."

Stuart and Jennifer looked at each other knowingly. "Do you have a picture of Mohammed?" Jennifer asked.

"Yes," Mrs. Mir responded and stood to go into the other room. When she returned, she handed the picture to Stuart, who in turn, offered it to Jennifer. Jennifer took it and stared. She nodded her head slowly in assent as Stuart looked at her questioningly. Jennifer understood his look and went over to talk to the children.

"Mrs. Mir," Stuart explained softly. "Mohammed was killed in an operation to rescue my wife, Jennifer, who was kidnapped by terrorists. We believe that Mohammed was as much a victim as Jennifer was. They used him to attempt to harm Jennifer; all the while, they were threatening to harm his family."

Mrs. Mir again became tearful as her husband attempted to comfort her. "He would never harm her," Mr. Mir whispered. "He tried to stop his twin sister from being violated and killed. He told us he was going to join their group in order to kill the leader and as many members as possible."

"He was caught in the cross fire," Stuart said, hoping that it would alleviate their fears. "He fell onto my wife as he was shot while the culprits were motioning for him to rape her, but he didn't rape her," Stuart said as gently as possible. "They were threatening that you would be killed if he didn't comply."

The Mirs held each other and cried. They were saying something in Arabic that Jennifer couldn't understand, but it might have been prayers. She continued reading the small book she had taken from her bag to the children. The Mirs were like that for a long time. Jennifer began reading another book to the twins. Finally, Mr. Mir looked up and asked Stuart, "What happened to his body?"

Stuart sat down across from them. "He was washed, shrouded,

and buried at sea facing Mecca," Stuart explained, hoping they would finally be a peace with his disappearance. "An imam recited prayers over him," Stuart lied, knowing it would bring them comfort. "He left you a gift though," Stuart continued. He motioned for Jennifer to come sit beside him. Jennifer gave the book to the children, who continued looking at the pictures, and kneeled down by Stuart's chair.

The Mirs looked up with hopeful eyes. Jennifer pulled a picture out of her bag and held it up for the Mirs to see. Mrs. Mir gasped after looking at the picture. She pointed to Sammi and Yara as she was speaking to Stuart. She began to cry again, only this time they were tears of joy.

"She says they look exactly like Mohammed and his sister when they were younger," Stuart translated to Jennifer.

"Would they like to meet them?" Jennifer asked.

"I've asked them to bring their kids to Jeddah and stay the weekend at the hotel with us," Stuart told her. "They can bring their suits, and we can hang out at the pool."

"Sounds perfect!" Jennifer agreed and smiled at the Mirs, who smiled back. What started out as a weekend to get to know one another ended up as a lifetime of friendship. Each year, Stuart, Jennifer, and the children visited their family in Mecca. After ten years, the Mirs received work visas and moved to America so that their children could finish high school and college in the States. Twenty years later, they all became U.S. citizens and raised their families within twenty miles of one another. Stuart continued working for Reuters, and Jennifer, Mrs. Mir, and Yara began a successful blog about raising independent multiple-birth siblings called NAOMI (Numbers Always Overlook My Individualism).

Henry Carter finally joined his Naomi after having daily discussions with her following her death. Stuart gladly wrote the obituary for *Reuters*, which was picked up by the *Times*. The final paragraph went as follows:

For Henry Carter, love did not die. It was the ray of light that could not be extinguished even in death. It continues to shine in the face of his beloved child, grandchildren, and great grandchildren, who will carry on his legacy. Henry Carter was a religious man, in that he lived a life that was pure in action, and he kept himself unspotted from the world. For Henry, death is not the end of his journey but a new beginning with his beloved Naomi in his immortal life. May all of us be so endeavored to seek out our hope of eternal life.

Stuart Jones, editor

The End

NOTES

1 Benjamin Franklin, "Letter to Ezra Stiles, March 9, 1790," Packard Humanities Institute: The Papers of Benjamin Franklin, https://franklinpapers.org/framedVolumes.jsp.

2 Thomas Jefferson, "From Thomas Jefferson to Elbridge Gerry, 26 January 1799," Founders Online, National Archives, https://founders.archives.gov/documents/Jefferson/01-30-02-0451.

3 George Washington, "Farewell Address," 1796.

4 John Adams and Charles Francis Adams, *Works: With a Life of the Author* (Boston:Little, Brown and Co., 1854) 229.

5 Barack Obama, "Remarks for Iftar Dinner, The White House, August 10, 2012" https://obamawhitehouse.archives.gov/the-press-office/2012/08/10/remarks-president-iftar-dinner.

6 Victor E. Frankl, *Man's Search For Meaning* (Rider, 2008) 94.

ACKNOWLEDGMENTS

I would like to thank the following individuals for their expertise and knowledge who have helped with the articles and conversations that took place in this fictional work. First, thanks to my friend Libby Stapleton who helped with editing. Her feedback was important in making this story more readable. Thanks to Maia and Eric Strinden and Gary Smith for their input, which helped clarify some of the events. Thanks also goes to Jag Aggarwal, Sunny Dharod, and the friends at Shikara Prabha Hindu Temple and Cultural Center of Kansas City for helping me understand the basics of Sanatana Dharma. I also want to thank Rabbi Javier Cattapan for his time and instruction about Judaism. Finally, I would like to acknowledge the groups and individuals found online:

Theological works of the late Father William G. Most and the Eternal Word Television Network
The Billy Graham Evangelistic Association
Jamaal Diwan, *A Brief Introduction to Islam*
Islamic Center of Pittsburgh
WhyIslam.org
Temple Buddhist Center Kansas City
Tricycle: The Buddhist Review

Encyclopedia Britannica
Chabad.org
Dennis Prager
Midwest Sikh Gudwara

This story is fiction, but the religion is pure.

ABOUT THE AUTHOR

Jane Doe first imagined the story, *Inside Religion*, several years ago as she was putting the final touches on her first book, *The Surgeon*. Now retired, Doe is an active member of her church who is enjoying sharing her new writing life adventure with her husband of forty-plus years, dogs, and grandchildren.

Printed in the United States
by Baker & Taylor Publisher Services